A TEENY TINY HALLOWEEN

By Lauren L. Wohl

Pictures by Henry Cole

PERSNICKETY PRESS

Designed by Hans Teensma, Impress

CPSIA Tracking Label Information
Production Location: Guangdong, China
Production Date: 4/15/2017
Batch Number: 79018

Library of Congress Cataloging-in-Publication
Data available.

ISBN: 978-1-943978-02-1
       978-1-943978-20-5

Manufactured in China

10 9 8 7 6 5 4 3 2 1

Persnickety Press

Persnickety Press
120A North Salem Street
Apex, NC 27502
Persnickety-Press.com

For Geoff who will always be
our best Halloween treat.

— L. L. W.

For S. F. M.

— H. C.

There is a teeny tiny woman who lives
in a teeny tiny house in a very big forest.

About this time every year, when the weather grows cool, the teeny tiny woman has a problem that is not so teeny tiny.

The wind comes howling
through the trees, and the leaves
fall,

fall,

fall …

until the teeny tiny house
is buried from the ground
to the roof.

Inside, the teeny tiny house
is dark as midnight.
It is, to be sure, a teeny tiny
bit scary.

"Oh, who will save me?" cries the
teeny tiny woman **in her** teeny tiny voice.
No one hears her.

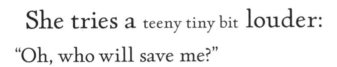

She tries a teeny tiny bit louder:
"Oh, who will save me?"

Then, one more time,
as loud as she can:
"Oh, who will save me?"
Still no one comes.

What to do? The teeny tiny woman opens a teeny tiny drawer and takes out a teeny tiny teaspoon. She taps it on the window over her teeny tiny table.

Tap   Tap   Tap.   But no one comes.

"I'm going to have to tap louder than that," says the teeny tiny woman to herself.

She reaches into the drawer again and grabs her biggest wooden mixing spoon.

Tap.

Tap.

Tap.

Still no one comes.

How can she make more noise? The teeny tiny woman
looks around. She opens her cupboard doors.
"Aha," she says in her teeny tiny voice. "I will bang my pots
and pans together. Someone is sure to hear that!"
She clangs her soup pot and her fry pan together.
Not loud enough.

She pulls out her cookie sheets — all three
—and crashes them together.
Nothing.
"Now what?" the teeny tiny woman wonders.
"Hmmmm." Then, looking at her cookie sheets
and her wooden spoon, she has an idea...

She takes a teeny tiny bowl from her teeny tiny cupboard, and she mixes up sugar and butter and flour and eggs with just the teeniest tiniest dash of vanilla and a teeny tiny mountain of chocolate chips.

She plops teeny tiny spoonfuls
of batter on her cookie sheet
and carries the tray to the oven.

While the cookies bake, an orange cat, a ghost, and a witch are walking in the forest near the teeny tiny house.

"Sniff. Sniff," the cat says.

"I smell cookies," the witch announces.

"Where is that delicious smell coming from?" the ghost asks.
All they see covering the forest floor are leaves,
	and twigs,
		and pine needles,
			and more leaves.

But wait! One pile of leaves is in the shape of a house. They begin to dig.

The cat on all fours
kicks away the dry
leaves: crackle, crackle.

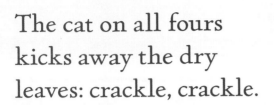

The witch sweeps leaves
away with her broom:
swoosh, swish.

And the ghost fans them
away with his billowing
sleeves: whooooo, whooooo.

Inside the teeny tiny house, the teeny tiny woman puts on her teeny tiny potholder glove and takes the cookies from the oven. They are golden and melty and gooey.

"This may be my best batch ever,"
she says in her teeny tiny voice.
"Much better than last year's."
She carries the tray to the teeny tiny table
near the teeny tiny window.

Outside the smell is so luscious and tempting that the cat, the witch and the ghost dig even faster.

Soon they uncover a teeny tiny chimney.
They dig faster still and discover the roof of a teeny tiny house.

"It's a teeny tiny house," the witch says.
They dig some more. They see the
teeny tiny door, push all the leaves away,
and knock.

Thump.

Thump.

Thump.

The teeny tiny woman takes three teeny tiny steps toward the door. She takes a deep breath, and she asks, loud as she can: "Who's there?"

"Did you hear something?"
    the ghost asks.
"Maybe," the witch says.
The cat knocks one more time,
    and all three shout

"TRICK OR TREAT!"

The teeny tiny woman claps her
teeny tiny hands.

She opens the
teeny tiny door.

There is a cat, and a witch, and a ghost.
But the teeny tiny woman is not the teeniest
bit scared.

She smiles her warmest teeny tiny smile, and in her happiest voice, bellows: "WELCOME, I'VE BEEN WAITING FOR YOU!"

Then all four sit down and eat the
teeny tiny chocolate chip cookies.
YUM.
YUM.
YUM.

Sebastian Smee

LUCIAN FREUD

TASCHEN

HONG KONG KÖLN LONDON LOS ANGELES MADRID PARIS TOKYO

FRONT COVER:
Portrait of Her Majesty the Queen, 2000/01
Oil on canvas, 23.5 x 15.2 cm
The Royal Collection

BACK COVER:
Lucian Freud in his studio, 2000
Photograph by Bruce Bernard
© Estate of Bruce Bernard

PAGE 1:
Self-Portrait, Reflection, 2002
Oil on canvas, 66 x 50.8 cm
Private collection

PAGE 2:
Lucian Freud in his studio, 2005
Photograph by David Dawson
© David Dawson, courtesy of Hazlitt Holland-Hibbert

To stay informed about upcoming TASCHEN titles, please request
our magazine at www.taschen.com/magazine or write to TASCHEN America,
6671 Sunset Boulevard, Suite 1508, USA-Los Angeles, CA 90028, contact-us@taschen.com, Fax: +1-323-463-4442.
We will be happy to send you a free copy of our magazine which is filled with information about all of our books.

© 2007 TASCHEN GmbH
Hohenzollernring 53, D–50672 Köln
www.taschen.com

© for the works of Lucian Freud: © Lucian Freud
© for the work of Edvard Munch: © VG Bild-Kunst, Bonn 2007

Project management: Petra Lamers-Schütze, Cologne
Editing, layout and typesetting: Lioba Waleczek, Cologne
Cover design: Claudia Frey, Cologne
Production: Martina Ciborowius, Cologne

Printed in Germany
ISBN 978-3-8228-5805-9

Contents

6
Beginnings

18
Closing In

30
Freud and Realism

36
Stretching Out

54
Biology

70
Realism as Theatre

92
Chronology

Beginnings

Lucian Freud is a painter of the body at rest. He is, as he likes to remind people, a biologist. He paints, draws and etches heads and bodies – predominantly the human kind, but frequently the animal kind. His interest is in truth-telling. But he brings to this apparently straightforward purpose an extraordinary sensitivity to what is involved in occupying a body: the sensation, the emotion, the intelligence, the bloom, the inevitable dissipation.

All this he refuses to think about in general terms. Rather, he has wanted to set down very specific truths about what it is like to occupy this particular body in this particular situation over this particular period of time. In the pursuit of this ambition, he has produced works that, in art historical as well as (inevitably) in human terms, are unprecedented.

"You cannot be aware enough," he has said. "I've always thought that biology was a great help to me and perhaps even having worked from animals was a help. I thought through observation I could make something into my own that might not have been seen or noticed or noted in that way before." For many decades now, the "situation" has been deliberately limited: it is the painter's studio. "My work is purely autobiographical," Freud has said. "It is about myself and my surroundings. It is an attempt at a record. I work from people that interest me, and that I care about and think about, in rooms that I live in and know." The period of time, too, has been relatively constant: Freud works slowly and, depending on size and other variables, his paintings can take between three and eighteen months.

But there have been few limits on the range of bodies or on the kinds of intimacy to which Freud has been willing – indeed avid – to respond. Interest in the person depicted has been the only prerequisite. In most cases, the stronger the interest, the better. "I paint people, not because of what they are like, not exactly in spite of what they are like, but how they happen to be." He has painted lovers and close friends, children and grandchildren, businessmen and fellow artists, writers and royalty, the notorious and the anonymous. "I don't think there's any kind of feeling that you have to leave out," he has said. And yet he is ruthless about omitting the exaggerated or false kind.

People often take the evidence in Freud's paintings of intense scrutiny over a long duration for a form of cruelty. But his notoriously "cruel" gaze is in truth something much more complicated and, in the end, liberating – not only from

Three-Legged Horse, 1937
Sandstone, height c. 56 cm
Private collection

At once condensed and attenuated, this horse (one of whose legs later broke off) was sculpted from sandstone when Freud was fifteen. Its appearance is ungainly, thwarted, intensely involved with itself, eliciting surges of intimacy and fascination.

PAGE 6:
Landscape with Birds, 1940
Oil on panel, 39.5 x 32.3 cm
Private collection

Box of Apples in Wales, 1939
Oil on canvas, 59.7 x 74.9 cm
Private collection

To look from the side-planks of the wooden
crate – precursors to Freud's later studio floorboards – to the pile of apples and on to the
meandering ridge lines of the mountain behind
is to sense what Freud seemed already convinced
of: that everything, attended to with sufficient
concentration, takes on a life of its own.

received ideas about beauty, but from the whole habit of sentimentality and pro-
jection that has characterised images of the human body throughout history.

In human terms, Freud's development as a painter has been, in part, a story
of affinities pursued, connections deepened. But it has also been, in aesthetic
terms, a tale of difficulties overcome, mannerisms unsettled, facility resisted.
"There's such a thing as, through working, having such a knowledge and profi-
ciency that you're free-wheeling," he once said. "Whereas I want to do things
that are really taxing."

"If his concentrated interest were to falter," wrote his friend, the painter Frank
Auerbach, "he would come off the tightrope; he has no safety net of manner.
Whenever his way of working threatens to become a style, he puts it aside like a
blunted pencil and finds a procedure more suited to his needs."

Freud is ferociously unsentimental, and permanently on guard against the
possibility that in his art he might be indulgent toward his subject matter. But
he certainly is one of the most profoundly attentive artists of all time. All the
qualities in his art, finally, come from this.

Lucian Freud was born in the last month of 1922. He was the second son of
Ernst Freud, an architect who, as a student, had practised as an artist in a style

derived from the Vienna Secession. Ernst was himself the youngest son of Sigmund Freud, the father of psychoanalysis. "I like the anarchic idea of coming from nowhere," Freud has said, "but I think that's probably because I had a very steady childhood." The family home was in an affluent area of Berlin near the Tiergarten. There was a maid, a cook and a governess, and summers were spent in a house on the Baltic. His mother Lucie's father, a grain merchant, owned an estate near Potsdam; it was there that Lucian first fell in love with horses.

As a child, Freud spent much of his time drawing, and with evident pride. There were prints by Hokusai and Dürer hanging in the home. Sigmund Freud, who came to Berlin from time to time for medical treatment, brought Lucian prints by Brueghel and an illustrated copy of *The Arabian Nights*. They both liked *Max and Moritz,* the antic, prank-filled comic strip by Wilhelm Busch that dated back to Sigmund's childhood. Did Sigmund Freud have much of an influence on his early years? Freud remembers his grandfather being "marvellously understanding and amused" about his developing ambitions to be an artist. In later years, he always claimed not to have read much of his grandfather's work, and yet he speaks of him with fondness and a certain protectiveness. "You know how laughter often seals your memory of someone?" he said. "He made me laugh a lot."

At the end of the summer of 1933, months after Hitler seized power, Freud's family emigrated to England. Unlike subsequent waves of Jewish emigrants, they were not refugees; they were able to take their possessions with them. Freud was

Hospital Ward, 1941
Oil on canvas, 25.4 x 35.5 cm
Duchess of Devonshire

The boy's eyes are wide and implacable, his mouth a long, lippy, horizontal slit stretched out at one end. Like so many of Freud's early subjects, the painting has the force of a boy's daydreams pressurised into being by reality; reality remembered or reality observed – at this point, it did not matter.

sent to boarding school in Devon with his brothers. The school, Dartington, was progressive. Freud, a recalcitrant student of English, made a point of avoiding classes, which were voluntary anyway, and revelled in his reputation as a wild boy more at ease with animals than other children. He would often sleep in the stables with the horses. In the mornings, he says, he rode the friskiest ones to tire them out for those who rode them later on.

Two years later, after his brothers had already been sent on to more conventional schools, Freud was moved to Bryanston, a 'public' (i.e. private) boys' school, where he became more serious about his art but, if anything, even less serious about his studies. He tried painting, along with pottery and sculpture. From sandstone, he carved a sculpture of a three-legged horse (ill. p.7). Freud abandoned sculpture after only a few more attempts. But his horse has an emotional inwardness and a powerfully concentrated emphasis on anatomical particulars that anticipates much of his work to come.

Others saw merit in it, too. Freud's father used it to secure a place for the boy at the Central School of Arts and Crafts in Holborn. He attended for a time, but his experience there does not seem to have been profitable. When Bernard Meninsky, an esteemed teacher of generations of English artists, undertook to teach him to draw, he played truant from his life classes, becoming proficient at ping-pong instead. Away from the art school, Freud explored what London had to offer in the way of bohemia. This, on the eve of war, translated to long hours at the Café Royal, an ornate bar redolent of *fin-de-siècle* decadence, and the Coffee An'.

Freud in his middle teens seems to have made an unforgettable impression on everyone he met. People "recognised his force immediately," wrote Lawrence Gowing: "fly, perceptive, lithe and with a hint of menace." John Richardson described him as "acutely self-conscious – shy and a touch exhibitionistic, yet resentful of the attention his exhibitionism sometimes triggered." Gowing was impressed, even at this stage, by a "coiled vigilance" in Freud, "and a sharpness in which one could imagine venom".

He met several people during this period who were to play an important role in his early development, among them Stephen Spender, Cyril Connolly and Peter Watson. Connolly was the editor of *Horizon,* the first publication to reproduce Freud's work (in 1939). Watson, who had a collection of modern art (Paul Klee, Juan Gris, Giorgio de Chirico) was its founder and backer. He later provided lodgings and other support for Freud.

War was imminent. In the circles he moved in, Freud, according to John Russell, "was the magnificent adolescent who seemed by his very presence not only to symbolise creativity but to hold the plague at bay … Everything was expected of him." It was Freud's determination, however, to run counter to expectation. And this persistent contrarian streak, an animal-like insistence on wriggling free, has never quite left him. If, for instance, he later made much of his lack of talent (he has claimed to have started out with "no natural aptitude for art whatsoever") such protestations need to be taken with a grain of salt. Certainly he was no Raphael. But he had been drawing all the time since coming to England, and there is plenty to show that he was someone to watch. What he seemed intent on finding was a way of proceeding that combined utmost concentration with a specificity, an exactitude, forced by curiosity and affinity alone. Anything that smacked of facility, any passage of generalised charm, was to be aggressively resisted.

Freud lasted just over a term at the Central School. At the suggestion of a girl he met at the Coffee An', he enrolled instead in the East Anglian School of Painting and Drawing at Dedham in Essex. Run by the painters Cedric Morris (ill. p.10)

Cedric Morris
Lucian Freud, 1940
Oil on canvas, 73.0 x 60.3 cm
London, Tate Britain

and Arthur Lett-Haines, this was a much more informal institution – not much more than a summer school – which disavowed formal teaching in favour of a sincere pursuit of individuality. Models were made available, and students could work in separate rooms. Above all, for Freud, there was the example of Cedric Morris, whose frank, determined and vibrantly gauche manner impressed him enormously. "He'd do the background and then the eyes and then he'd do the whole thing in one go and not touch it again. I thought Cedric was a real painter. Dense and extraordinary. Terrific limitations."

Meanwhile, Sigmund Freud died and war broke out. That autumn, Freud and David Kentish, a friend who had moved with him from Bryanston to the art school, took themselves off to a miner's cottage in Capel Curig in the north of Wales. There, for three months, they painted during the days and drew by lamplight in the cold evenings. Freud took with him some paintings he had already begun. One of them, *Box of Apples*, became *Box of Apples in Wales* (1939, ill. p. 8) when he added a background of bare Welsh mountains. When Stephen Spender joined Freud and Kentish in Wales after Christmas, Freud's sketchbook filled up with drawings remarkable for their air of concentrated mischief. Freud was quick

The Refugees, 1941/42
Oil on panel, 50.8 x 61 cm
Private collection

This painting is an identity parade of faces from the refugee community Freud had observed over several years. The influence of Cedric Morris is apparent in the flat look of the faces, the improvised simplicity of the composition (based on a newspaper photograph) and the curdled paint.

The Painter's Room, 1943/44
Oil on canvas, 62.2 x 76.2 cm
Private collection

Freud, who loved all things equine from an early
age, was given this stuffed zebra's head, which
he kept in his studio. The painting's combination
of wilfully disparate elements recalls, as Robert
Hughes has written, Lautréamont's passage
about the sewing machine and the umbrella on
an operating table. Freud later turned away from
this intriguing but rather mannered surrealism.
He said: "I think Lautréamont's umbrella and
sewing machine on an operating table was an
unnecessarily elaborate encounter. What could
be more surreal than a nose between two eyes?"

Jean Auguste Dominique Ingres
Monsieur de Norvins, 1811
Oil on canvas mounted on panel, 97.2 x 78.7 cm
London, National Gallery

The emphasis on line and emotional intensity
in Freud's paintings of the 1950s caused him to
be referred to as the "Ingres of Existentialism"
by Herbert Read (see pp. 19, 23, 71).

PAGE 15:
Boy on a Balcony, 1944/45
Conté and crayon, heightened with white,
53.3 x 35.5 cm
Private collection

One eye is slightly opened, without quite wanting to be, and a great nervous pressure is conveyed by his straightened forearm and clenched
fist. This image powerfully suggests the strain
of awareness, of being observed, as well as the
strain of scrutiny.

to reject the notion of a "disinterested eye"; rather, his lines went where he took
them. Often this was into a realm of private jokes and antic fancy. The sketchbook included many drawings of horses, studies inspired by El Greco, macabre
or fantastic imaginings ferociously set down, and a series of portraits of Spender.
The drawing was resolutely linear, the lines themselves slow, meandering, with
abrupt directional changes and no regard for composition or coherence. They
were at once predetermined and wholly unpredictable, like hairline cracks in a
rock face.

Over the next few years, Freud's work veered between minor triumphs of
compellingly original observation and moments where you detect a slightly
self-preening manner. The manner may have been borne of a desire to avoid
certain other kinds of mannerism – in particular, the vaguely indicated emo-
tions of English Neo-Romanticism – but it had its dangers. In Freud's early
work, there is little hint of the physicality and attention to volume that so de-
fines his mature work. And yet most of the themes that would later preoccupy
him emerge in these formative years: a concentration on the faces of people
he knows; close-in descriptions of heads, often with downcast eyes; the lives
of animals and plants; and various objects scrutinised at close quarters.

Freud preferred the literal to the abstract, drawing to painting, spiky linearity
to soothing curves, awkwardness to virtuosity. He believed that if something
worthwhile were going to emerge, it would be the result of concentration. That
hasn't changed – not in more than half a century. What did change – though
not for many years – was Freud's preference for drawn lines over all the vicissi-
tudes of oil paint. For the time being, wrote Lawrence Gowing, "drawing was
a defence against the received idea of painting… Painting presented itself as
drawing to Freud because any other medium seemed beyond him. He thought
the qualities that he admired in painting were far too removed for them ever
to bear fruit for him." Nonetheless, he admired Chaim Soutine's paintings of
dead animals (ill. p. 17); he was impressed by Joris-Karl Huysmans's essay on
Grünewald, and Van Gogh was an abiding inspiration. But as he said himself:
"My method was so arduous that there was no room for influence."

In 1941, feeling adventurous, Freud used some money he had won in a textile
design competition to go to Liverpool. There he signed on as an Ordinary Sea-
man on a Merchant Navy ship that sailed in convoy across the Atlantic and back.
The voyage, which lasted several months, added considerably to the legend that
thickened around Freud in London's bohemian circles, but it was tough on him.
The convoy came under attack on several occasions. Freud fared badly in the
freezing cold and fell ill with tonsillitis. Back in England, he was discharged from
the Merchant Navy, and had his tonsils out in a hospital at Ashbridge. When he
returned to art school, he painted *Hospital Ward* (1941, ill. p. 9), the convalescing
patient's head (based on the face of Peter Watson) flattened and seemingly col-
laged onto the pillow behind.

Determined to avoid any appearance of handmade "artiness", Freud set rules
for himself. He would never apply paint on top of paint. He would never touch
anything twice, and so on. The strongest works from this period, besides *Hospital Ward*, are *Landscape with Birds* (1940, ill. p. 6), a boyish reverie painted before
the Atlantic crossing, and *The Refugees* (1941/42, ill. p. 11). The sky in *Landscape
with Birds*, painted in ripolin enamel paint, has an accidentally curdled look, but
also a faceted, opalescent intensity, which provides a flattened, rhythmic back-
drop for Freud's ten airborne but floundering birds. Their pointed beaks and
spiky plumage rhyme with the stellated flowers and prickly twigs beneath.

Dead Heron, 1945
Oil on canvas, 49 x 74 cm
Private collection

The dead bird's feathered body is rendered with a sustained sensitivity to tonal variation and an unblinking fidelity to each bedraggled feather tip. The painting is a great instance of the actuality of a thing triumphing over any idea of it. The result? Not reality depleted but reality intensified.

Freud is a painter of disparities rather than concordances. In *The Refugees*, and whenever he has painted group portraits in the six decades subsequently, he shows himself more interested in each individual's separate existence than in the way the figures relate to each other. Each of the refugees is drawn to a completely different scale. Their faces, as in many of Freud's early portraits, look as if they have been pressed and smudged slightly to one side. But this pressurised effect is staunchly resisted by their strict outlines and beady, expressionless eyes.

At this stage, situations and literary imaginings still had a stronger hold over Freud than any specific connections with people. He moved in a milieu of poets and authors, and was cultivating an abiding interest in stories and poetry. In objects, too, he found a spring-loaded intensity redolent of Surrealism. Still things, concentrated upon, could be hinges for the imagination to turn on. Stillness, moreover, made outlines, textures, patterns and plumage easier to fix. And so Freud painted and drew still-lifes: a monkey corpse, a sleeping baby, a dead rabbit, cactuses and thistles, a lemon, an unripe tangerine, and dead birds, stuffed, laid out on tables or discarded in buckets.

He also made two superb drawings of a boy with downcast eyes. In one the boy wears no shirt; his eyes are closed and there is nothing distorted in his clear, open features. He is protected, despite his vulnerability, by obliviousness. In the next drawing, *Boy on a Balcony* (1944/45, ill. p. 15), the same boy, clothed now in shirt, tie and jacket, has been enveloped in an atmosphere of such intensity that it is impossible to tell whether its real source is internal or external. The contrast with the oblivion of the earlier picture is palpable.

Freud moved from Abercorn Place to a flat in Delamere Terrace, in Paddington, an area he was to stay in for the next thirty years. The area was run-down and shabby, and he had violent neighbours. "There was a sort of anarchic element of no-one working for anyone." He had his first solo show at the Lefevre Gallery in November 1944. Michael Ayrton, reviewing it for *The Spectator,* criticised Freud's drawing: "The human form defeats him because he does not observe it as he does dead birds." "His youthful mannerisms add up to a personality," wrote John Piper in *The Listener.* "Too many forms are depressed by having to deliver unimportant literary messages but he has a cultivated feeling for line, when he can be bothered with it, and a natural feeling for colour."

All this may not have touched Freud very much, but the exposure helped define for him what he did and did not want to be. A primitive – a boy wonder bound to childish affectation – he was determined not to be. Lawrence Gowing, writing of these early years, described Freud's determination "to be no-one and nothing except his own kind of painter, the ungovernably greedy, human kind … Painting has for him the character of his appetite, the preternaturally sharp-eyed appreciation which is also a kind of possessiveness."

One of the paintings in Freud's first show was *The Painter's Room* (1943/44, ill. pp. 12/13), which has long been regarded as the prime example of his early dalliance with Surrealism. Undoubtedly, with its red-striped zebra head coming in through a window, its top hat and red scarf on the floor, its battered couch and ailing palm, it has the look of an essay in poetic Surrealism. But Freud's affinity with Surrealism, rather than growing, reached its apogee in this work. There had been a large survey of Surrealist work in London before the war, and Freud was keen on de Chirico, some of Dalí and Miró. But, as he said, "I wanted things to look possible rather than irrational, if anything eliminating the surrealist look." Far from being concocted out of thin air, the zebra head, as contemporary photographs show, was a proud possession of the young artist. It was a gift from Lorna Wishart, who went on to buy the painting for fifty pounds.

"I think Lautréamont's umbrella and sewing machine on an operating table was an unnecessarily elaborate encounter," Freud later said, in a neat encapsulation of his feelings about Surrealism. "What could be more surreal than a nose between two eyes?" Wishart became Freud's first serious girlfriend. Two portraits of her sitting at a table were his attempt to convey "that she was the first person I was really caught up with." She was responsible for obtaining not only the zebra head but also a dead heron which was the subject of one of Freud's most powerful war-time pictures (ill. p. 16). The bird is splayed on a flat ochre surface (which may be a landscape; there is a hint of dawning sky at the left edge of the horizon); its heraldic presence seems to contradict its evident lifelessness.

Like many of his generation who had been cooped up in Britain during the war, Freud was eager to go abroad when the fighting finally stopped. With introductions from Peter Watson and money from his new dealer, the London Gallery, he went to Paris in the summer of 1946. From there he went to Greece, where John Craxton was living. He did not return until the following year. In Paris – then, and on subsequent trips – he met Picasso and became friendly with Giacometti. It is impossible to do any more than speculate on the effect such encounters had on Freud, who was by now in his mid-twenties. But he held both artists in the highest regard, and, in their different ways, Giacometti and Picasso provided models – of will, of conviction, of inventiveness, of lives exuberantly lived yet still revolving around the studio – that he was eager to emulate.

Chaim Soutine
Two Pheasants, c. 1919
Oil on canvas, 64.7 x 50.2 cm
Private collection

Closing In

Back in London in 1947 Freud met Kitty Garman, who sat for several of his most memorable early works. Kitty's mother was Lorna Wishart's eldest sister Kathleen; her father was the sculptor Jacob Epstein. She married Freud in the spring of 1948 and had a daughter by him, Annie, in July. Freud painted five head-and-shoulders portraits of Kitty in 1947/48, and an etching, *Ill in Paris*, in 1948. She was pregnant towards the end of this period, although there is only a drawing, *Mother and Baby* (1949), to indicate this.

How to account for the sudden, almost electrifying intensification of feeling in these portraits? A deepening emotional tie must be part of any answer – it is quite palpable. But these portraits also see Freud developing a new way to get across the kind of inwardness and emotional pressures he was so interested in. Looking at them, you feel Freud's earlier penchant for whim or fancy has been completely excised. Instead, the priority becomes a very fastidious, very consistent distribution of information across the surface of the picture.

The result is a surface tension for which Kitty's large, glassy, almond-shaped eyes become a sort of amplifying tautology. Whether she is looking at the viewer or away, her acute awareness of being scrutinised is impossible to miss. You feel the pressure of the artist's gaze amounting almost to a threat – not the threat of violence but certainly a threat to self-possession. "It seems impossible," Gowing wrote, "that she should not have been trembling." And yet, against the odds, Kitty maintains her self-possession and meets this scrutiny with an implied permission that is deeply intimate and, finally, implacable.

The masterpiece of the series is *Girl with a Kitten* (1947, ill. p. 18). In it, Kitty looms closer than in the others. The evenness of Freud's attention to her stray hairs, hand, eyes and sleeve, and to the kitten itself, contradicts the implication of emotional extremity, creating a self-sustaining tension. The combination of extreme pictorial composure and barely contained intensity brings to mind certain portraits by Ingres (ill. p. 14), an artist Freud has always loved. One thinks, for instance, of the simmering aggression in Ingres's portrait of Monsieur de Norvins in London's National Gallery, which Freud would have known well. The emotion is different but the intensity is not. Within a few years, introducing Freud's work at the Venice Biennale, Herbert Read was to dub him the "Ingres of Existentialism". The label stuck, making more or less sense at different times in Freud's career; but it was never more apt than during the period that began

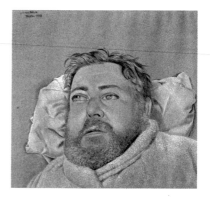

Christian Bérard, 1948
Black and white conté, 41 x 44 cm
Private collection

The dead-eyed weariness in Bérard's eyes, the asymmetry of his face and the sense of almost indecorous physical proximity prefigure Freud's mature works. Bérard died two months later, after a stroke.

PAGE 18:
Girl with a Kitten, 1947
Oil on canvas, 39.5 x 29.5 cm
Private collection

Kitty Garman, Freud's first wife, looks off to the side, but the kitten she grips in her right hand stares straight back at us, creating an unsettling geometry of gazes. Kitty's presence is magnificently imperious, like an Egyptian queen's, and yet she seems intensely vulnerable.

Father and Daughter, 1949
Oil on canvas, 91.5 x 45.7 cm
Private collection

Freud's neighbour, Henry Minton, and his
daughter are seen through the gap in a bead
curtain. The situation seems fraught with
discomfort, but what is noticeable is the dis-
cordance between the sitters, the completely
separate quality of both their appearance and
their gazes, despite their contact and kindred
relationship.

PAGE 20 TOP:
Girl with a White Dog, 1951/52
Oil on canvas, 76.2 x 101.6 cm
London, Tate Britain

The psychological force of the painting is intensified by the strange concordances and disparities
between human life and animal life: between a
canine ear and a human sleeve; between a snout
and a breast; between Kitty's big eyes and the
dog's squashed-looking face.

PAGE 20 BOTTOM:
Sleeping Nude, 1950
Oil on copper, 76.2 x 101.6 cm
Private collection

with the portraits of Kitty and ended in the mid-1950s, when other changes took place.

In the meantime, Freud produced, in his drawing of the epicurean set designer Christian Bérard, one of the great portrait drawings of the 20th century (1948, ill. p. 19) – an image that owes more than a little to Ingres. Some of Freud's other drawings from the time seem stuck in an original but rather illustrative mode; this was clearly a breakthrough.

Two paintings from the late 1940s are the first indication that, in the long haul, an interest in physical repose, in the self-revealing body, will win out over the challenge and intensity of wide-eyed stares and an atmosphere of melting pathos. One of them, *Sleeping Nude* (1950, ill. p. 20 bottom), is a coolly sensuous study of a sleeping woman, naked down to her waist, very much in the spirit of Ingres. If the painting is slightly too controlled, and unexpectedly decorous, it nevertheless points to a great maturing in Freud's ability (and willingness) to render volumes through subtle gradations of tone and colour. It also reveals a marvellous sensitivity to light. It is, however, in the second painting, *Girl with a White Dog* (1951/52, ill. p. 20 top), that Freud seems most himself. The girl is Kitty, and the animal was the second of a pair of dogs they kept together. Freud started off painting the first, which was black, but it was run over before the picture was finished, whereupon he replaced it with the white one.

The picture is one of Freud's greatest, though the marvel of it is difficult to describe. Two sentient beings stare out at us. The girl, in a dressing gown, reveals one of her breasts, which lolls from her chest like a third animal presence. Her hand cradles the other through her dressing gown. The dog seems more comfortable, but no less watchful. Again there is a great tension between challenge and submission: the challenge of discordant gazes, the submission of sitting. Compositionally, too, the painting is a great feat of organisation. The strong verticals and horizontals are sewn together by the diagonals that jut down as folds in the drapery and rise again through Kitty's arm. (Soon, mind you, Freud would return to the idea, dominant in his youth, that composing a picture meant falsifying it, pre-ordaining what should be unguessed-at and urgent. "Do you know there is something called picture-making?" he once said. "I think it is often simply fatigue. It rules out the hope of making something remarkable.")

During all these years, Freud liked to feel, as William Feaver wrote, "that he could move through society at will, flitting from place to place, dancing with a princess in nightclubs, going on a double-decker bus with Garbo, frequenting Soho, painting anyone from a newspaper seller or scene shifter to the Dowager Duchess of Devonshire, treating all as private individuals." This social manoeuvrability is not quite incidental to the work. In his painting, Freud has not deliberately sought out unremarkable people in order to make some broader point about ordinariness; nor has he sought out society's noteworthy. His subjects happen to be who they happen to be. Decisions about whom to paint next come down entirely to impulse – *his* impulse. And to that extent, the work is, as he insists, "autobiographical. It's all to do with hope and memory and sensuality and involvement, really."

By the time he painted *Girl with a White Dog,* Freud's relationship with Kitty was beginning to disintegrate. At the invitation of William Coldstream, he had taken up a position as tutor at the Slade School, although his appearances there were rare and unpredictable. Through Graham Sutherland, he met Francis Bacon. He also met, and in 1953 married, Caroline Blackwood.

Girl in Bed, 1952
Oil on canvas, 45.7 x 30.5 cm
Private collection

Caroline Blackwood was Freud's second wife. They married in 1953. Blackwood was a writer (she later married the American poet Robert Lowell) and the daughter of the 4th Marquis of Dufferin and Ava and his wife Maureen née Guinness, the brewery heiress. In an admiring article on Freud published in 1993, she said she had been "dismayed … as to why he needed to paint a girl, who at that point still looked childish, as so distressingly old. It is interesting to note that the many portraits he painted in the forties and fifties, in what is now considered his most romantic and gentle style, at the time were seen by many as shocking and violent and cruel."

PAGE 22:
Boy's Head, 1952
Oil on canvas, 21.6 x 15.9 cm
Private collection

Freud's interest in the slippage that can occur between bone, flesh and skin is evident here. Note the pronounced attention paid to the pressure of the boy's supporting hand on his cheek, the way it pulls muscle and skin and even mouth and nose out of alignment. Here again, there is a sense that one could not get closer without one's vision blurring.

A Young Painter, 1957/58
Oil on canvas, 40.8 x 39.4 cm
Private collection

Page 25:
Francis Bacon, 1952
Oil on copper, 17.8 x 12.8 cm
Whereabouts unknown

Freud and Bacon became friends in the 1950s.
Bacon's eyes are downcast but still visible, so
that, rather than being met by a wide-eyed,
challenging stare, we are pushed into close
proximity with a man attending to his own
thoughts. Where the left side of his face is relatively lifeless, the right side seems animated,
even aggressive. Our reproduction shows the
painting in original size.

The intensity in Freud's pictures during this period was in part a function of
scale. Control was paramount. Freud wanted to convey an almost febrile absorp-
tion in his subjects. So it made sense for him to work at a scale much smaller than
life size. Anything larger might have meant a loss of control. But he soon felt the
limitations of this approach, and so in several of the best pictures of this period
you can sense a tension brewing. On the one hand, Freud ratchets up the intensity, in part through a painstaking, uniform fidelity to detail. On the other, he
becomes increasingly interested in his sitters' three-dimensional presence and,
in particular, volumetric idiosyncrasies such as sagging skin, bone structure,
bunches of muscle, pouches of fat, dimples, light-reflecting oils, pockmarks and
other blemishes. He wants to get us closer to all these things. Even the organisation of his images aims at this: heads are cropped so that they fill the frame, odd
angles are introduced, and protective barriers between subject and viewer are removed. The objective, almost alien, intensity of the portraits of Kitty is gradually
replaced by a less contrived, though no less unsentimental, breathing, proximate
presence.

Freud's portrait of Bacon (ill. p. 25), which was stolen from a Berlin gallery
and remains unaccounted for to this day, is a superb example of this new approach. It is a small painting on copper. Freud spent three months on it. He and
Bacon sat knee-to-knee. Thus, Bacon's pear-shaped face fills the frame, lending
the image an unlikely monumentality. But the sense of inwardness is electrifying.
The left half of Bacon's face is in shadow and fairly uneventful. On the right,
although the quality of attention remains even, the contrast is tremendous.
Everything seems animated, potential, at boiling point. From the bottom up we
notice: a slight asymmetry – almost an arrogant curl – in the upper lip; a pouchy
swelling at the corner of the mouth; a sheen of sweat or oil around the slopes of
his nose; and, of course, the striking horizontal S-curve of his eyebrow matching
the vertical S-curve of a stray lick of hair.

In the same year that he painted Bacon, Freud produced *Girl in Bed* (1952,
ill. p. 23), a beautiful portrait of Caroline Blackwood from the point of view of
someone sharing her bed. The image is a world away from the portraits of Kitty.
Kitty's cool pallor has been replaced by golden skin tones, freckles, a reddish nose,
and suggestions of veins beneath the skin. With the closer observation, the more
ample description, comes a deepening sense of attachment and various somatic
associations, including touch and implied movement. And yet the vulnerability
remains the same.

Which other artists were producing images like this? There weren't any. There
was a prevailing drive towards abstraction on both sides of the Atlantic. Even figurative artists were preoccupied with the expressive potential of semi-abstracted
forms, distortion, various painterly freedoms. In terms of approach, Freud's closest cousins in these years may have been Netherlandish painters such as Van Eyck
and Robert Campin. But as his interest in volumes grew, and the intimacy of his
relationships deepened, the tight surfaces and exacting control of Freud's method
began to seem a limitation.

"My eyes were completely going mad, sitting down and not being able to
move," he told William Feaver. "Small brushes, fine canvas. Sitting down used
to drive me more and more agitated. I felt I wanted to free myself from this way
of working." *Hotel Bedroom* (1954), a moody set-piece showing Freud standing
watchfully in the background as Caroline Blackwood lies in bed, was, he said,
"the last painting where I was sitting down; when I stood up I never sat down
again." It was also one of the last works Freud painted with a fine, sable brush.

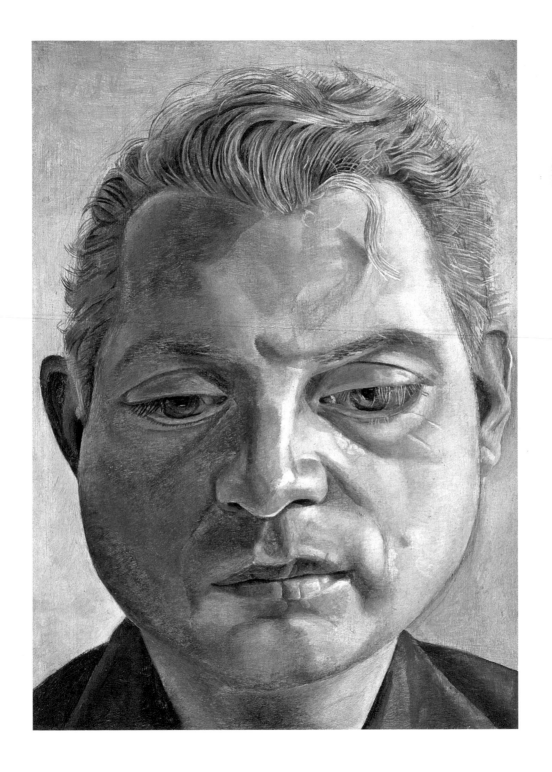

From this point on, he worked with thicker, hogs-hair brushes, amplifying his touch, making each contact between brush and canvas more of a gamble.

Francis Bacon played a critical role in the changes that now began to take place. Their friendship had an effect on Freud that was both personal and artistic. Bacon lived life on the brink: he courted risk; he was immensely charming. He was already producing works that had massive psychological force. They were violent, explosive, fuelled by risk. "He talked," said Freud, "about packing a lot of things into one single brushstroke, which amused and excited me, and I realised that it was a million miles from anything I could ever do." Freud was losing patience with his own methods, and he glimpsed possibilities in Bacon's approach. He pushed himself accordingly. Without succumbing to generalisation, he broadened his handling, setting certain brushstrokes free from specific description. "If you look at the forms," he said, referring to the tight paintings of the late 1940s and early 1950s, "it is clear that some of them want to be liberated." For the most part, this liberation took place very slowly. Freud contrived to maintain an overall evenness of attention. But, expanding his repertoire of painterly effects, he worked hard to convey the deep structure of his sitters' faces. In portraits such as *Woman in a White Shirt* (1956/57), and *A Young Painter* (1957/58, ill. p. 24), he seemed to be working from the inside out, disregarding outlines in favour of the planes and volumes that vie and jostle within them. Many of the forms of the face – bunches of muscle, fatty tissue, bone and surging blood – work at cross-purposes to each other, he realised, and it became his task to get this over in paint.

Pregnant Girl (1960/61, ill. p. 27) is a masterpiece of the period, in part because the intimacy it conveys is extreme, but also because the focus on a flourishing body, rather than the detailed scrutiny of a face, seems to have allowed Freud more freedom to loosen up form and volume. The three strands of muscle and tendon that rise from the girl's shoulder and converge in her neck suggest nothing that is not based in observation, but the brushstrokes they are conveyed with are remarkably broad and lively. Line becomes shape becomes volume in a dance of ambiguity that nevertheless feels as sincerely truthful, as locked in place, as a landscape by Cézanne.

In other portraits from this fascinating, inconsistent period, Freud pushes the loosening up process further. He also comes at his subjects – a baby, a woman, a man with his knees drawn up on a chair – from an array of different angles, so that the sense of things coming untethered applies not just to the forms but also to the ambiguous, unsettled way they occupy the space around them.

"I felt more discontented than daring," Freud later said of this period. "It wasn't that I was abandoning something dear to me, more that I wanted to develop something unknown to me."

Figure with Bare Arms, 1962
Oil on canvas, 91.5 x 91.5 cm
Viscountess Lambton / The Lambton Trustees

Red-Haired Man on a Chair, 1962/63
Oil on canvas, 91.5 x 91.5 cm
Private collection

Freud and Realism

In his 1988 monograph on Freud, Robert Hughes described him as "the greatest living realist painter". It is a formulation that has been used repeatedly since – and not without justification: the realist label has the virtue of placing Freud in a tradition that leads from Rembrandt and Velázquez through to Chardin, Constable, Corot, Courbet and Degas – all artists he reveres. But in some ways, the term is an uneasy fit.

In fact, it has never been adequate. Even Courbet, at the start of his *Realist Manifesto*, was moved to say: "The title of Realist was imposed on me ... Never have titles given an accurate idea of things ..." Of course, in ordinary discussion, 'realism' is usually used to convey an interest in empirical facts, including those that may be regarded as unpleasant or challenging. Philosophically, it implies an honest acceptance of limitations, one that goes hand in hand with a suspicion of false feeling and lofty ideals. All of this fits neatly enough with Freud. And yet, taken together, its explanatory force is limited. Most obviously, it ignores the element of surprise or revelation in his pictures, the disturbance they cause. It may also underestimate the force of what they *refuse* to do.

Some people regard realism's premise – that reality is something a painter might credibly reproduce – as naïve or conservative. But the idea of realism in its heyday was always more expansive than people give it credit for. Courbet, for instance, was the most unconventional painter of his time. In his *Realist Manifesto,* he spoke of wanting to create an art that existed "apart from any preconceived system and without biases..." He was echoed by Edmond Duranty, who described realism as an "attack upon convention, [upon] any kind of school". (Freud, too, hates schools: "The term 'like-minded' is something I'd run a mile from," he has said.) Duranty called for paintings to contain a "frank and complete expression of individuality" but also to express a "love of truth". The two things were not to be regarded as incompatible. Zola, more pithily, spoke of the work of art as "a corner of nature seen through a temperament".

In other words, far from striving to attain the impossible and, in the end, banal goal of a completely objective art, great 19th-century realists like Courbet followed their own subjective impulses. Emphasising subjectivity was crucial since, for the realist, reality could not be universalised. It was, as Linda Nochlin has written, "bound to a concrete situation at a given moment of time. It is what it is, when it is, where it is, nothing more."

Man's Head (Self-Portrait), 1963
Oil on canvas, 53.3 x 50.8 cm
Manchester, Whitworth Art Gallery,
University of Manchester

PAGE 30:
Girl in a Fur Coat, 1967
Oil on canvas, 61 x 51 cm
Fukuoka, Fukuoka Sogo Bank, Ltd.

Interior with Hand Mirror (Self-Portrait), 1967
Oil on canvas, 25.5 x 17.8 cm
Private collection

Just like his realist forebears, Freud has a horror of rhetoric and of the impulse to universalise. "I think the most boring thing you can say about a work of art is that it's 'timeless,'" he once said. "That induces a kind of panic in me. It's almost like political speech – it doesn't apply to anyone. The idea that something's wrong if the work gives off a feeling of being tied to the moment is crazy."

But of course, despite Courbet's stated aversion to rhetoric, *his* realism – like Zola's in literature – also involved a social programme, an ambitious reach across the whole of society which was highly political in both intention and effect. Freud's portraiture, by contrast, completely jettisons this aspect of 19th-century realism. Yes, he paints people from every section of society – from the Queen to bookmakers, fellow artists and criminals. But he makes no claim for his choices beyond private impulse. His interest is not in the political or even the social but

Interior with Plant, Reflection Listening
(Self-Portrait), 1967/68
Oil on canvas, 121.8 x 121.8 cm
Private collection

Gustave Courbet
The Bathers, 1853
Oil on canvas, 227 x 193 cm
Montpellier, Musée Fabre

merely in the artistic, human possibilities afforded by each of his subjects' specific presences. "Nothing ever stands in for anything … Nobody is representing anything. Everything is autobiographical, and everything is a portrait, even if it's a chair."

Rather than scouring society for external, 'typical' subjects, Freud works in a setting that is overwhelmingly internal – almost never beyond his back garden – and almost always from people he knows. Inimitable people. "Whom else can I hope to portray with any degree of profundity?" Although he is bound to the studio he sees no limitation in this. "My idea of travel is downward travel really," he told William Feaver. "Getting to know where you are, better, and exploring feelings that you know more deeply. I always think that thing 'knowing something by heart' gives you a depth of possibility which is more potential than seeing new sights, however marvellous and exciting they are."

Despite all this, Courbet remains a touchstone. Courbet was, after all, one of art history's most powerful acts of self-invention, a sustained example of gaucheness overcome – or augmented – by sheer will. Freud speaks admiringly of his "shamelessness". And it's true: one cannot look at Courbet's extraordinary nudes (ill. p. 34) and keep in mind his political themes. Instead, one marvels at the headlong commitment, the lack of self-censorship and, yes, the "shamelessness". The same applies to the oak tree he painted at Flagey or the greyhounds which belonged to the Count de Choiseul. In his self-portraiture, too, one detects a sense of theatre, mixed in with a brutal honesty and sly self-awareness, that is immediately recognisable in Freud's own self-portraits (of which more later).

For Freud, the most important aspect of Courbet's work is not, perhaps, his 'realism', but his material involvement with the paint itself. At the heart of this involvement is an attitude to the business of getting it down on canvas, an attitude all to do with intensity and effectiveness – "like people shouting and using any old word because somehow the way they are shouting will get through", as Freud has put it. "If you know what you want you can use almost anything. An ungrammatical shout is no less clear. It's to do with the urgency."

In the end, 19th-century realism was predicated on knowing – on our ability to know about things and people. It was an outgrowth, after all, of 19th-century positivism. Freud's painting is subtly different. It is predicated on a form of truth-telling which makes room for the honesty of not-knowing. And this is one of the ways in which he turns 19th-century realism on its head.

Indeed, one of Freud's great contributions to the whole idea of portraiture has been to shift it away from the presumption of knowing – of illustrating personality traits or 'penetrating character'. Instead, his work is about degrees of affinity. "When you find things moving, the desire to find out more lessens rather," he once said. "Rather like when in love with someone, you don't want to meet the parents."

Although his portraits take candour to new levels, and although he scrutinises his models with unflinching intensity, he does not presume to know his subjects definitively. Instead, by showing his models asleep or with closed eyes, by rejecting symbols and storytelling, by keenly observing their self-modulating presence over hours and hours of sitting – indeed, in a thousand different ways – he powerfully registers their unknowability. He is, as Augie March claims to be at the end of Bellow's great novel *The Adventures of Augie March,* "a sort of Columbus of those near-at-hand", approaching his subjects through the "immediate *terra incognita* that spreads out in every gaze".

Reflection with Two Children (Self-Portrait), 1965
Oil on canvas, 91.5 x 91.5 cm
Madrid, Museo Thyssen-Bornemisza

Freud sees himself in a mirror placed on the floor,
his painting tools hidden from view, his head
awkwardly foreshortened against the reflected ceiling.
His expression seems sly, challenging.

Stretching Out

As the 1960s progressed, Freud's truth-telling capacity deepened, just as his refusal to editorialise or feign knowing became more pronounced. His painting grew gradually richer, more pliable and responsive, the paint's textures interacting in ever more surprising ways with the definition of forms. *Naked Child Laughing* (1963, ill. p. 36) demonstrates the expansion beautifully. The work is small – just 34 by 28 cm – but it is Freud's first full-body nude. The model, Freud's daughter, sits on a couch, legs jack-knifed on the seat, chin in hand, elbow on wrist, wrist on hip. The architecture of limbs and joints is itself eloquent: the girl looks coy but comfortable.

But it is really the paint that communicates everything. The girl's whole body is made to issue from broadly handled passages across the chromatic range from red and brown to white, and across all the tones. The light, mind you, is strong and uniform; nothing is lost in shadow; there is no rhetoric of mystification. Broad strokes convey the articulation of forearm, wrist and knuckle with a freedom that suggests the excitement of deep engagement rather than the theatricality of expressionism. A long thin swipe of white gets over the girl's gleaming, bony shin, while thick zigzags of dark brown convey the hair falling around her hand. The artist's refusal to proceed according to conventional expectation, and the consequent sense of risk, are enthralling.

Do we need to know why the child is laughing? Or indeed that she is Freud's daughter? Not in the least. What matters is that we register her presence with the greatest possible immediacy, and from this flows all the work's emotion: the surprise of intimacy, the confusing oscillation between vulnerability and unguarded ease, the inexplicable human gorgeousness. Ironically, the closest thing in art to Freud's *Naked Child Laughing* is probably Edvard Munch's *Weeping Nude* (1913, ill. p. 37). It is not so much that the forms resemble each other (although they do); it is to do, rather, with the treatment, the sense of conviction, the intensity. These are the things one registers and responds to – not some imagined story about why a child might be either weeping or laughing.

Freud's development from this point on is all about finding the means to register his subjects' specificity. "I think a great portrait has to do with the way it is approached," he said. "If you look at Chardin's animals, they're absolute portraits. It's to do with the feeling of individuality and the intensity of the regard and the focus on the specific. So I think portraiture is an attitude. Painting things

Edvard Munch
Weeping Nude, 1913
Oil on canvas, 110.5 x 135 cm
Oslo, Munch Museum

PAGE 36 :
Naked Child Laughing, 1963
Oil on canvas, 34 x 28 cm
Private collection

This small work is Freud's first full-body nude. The model is Freud's daughter, the first of many naked portraits of his children.

Cyclamen, 1964
Oil on canvas, 45.7 x 49.2 cm
Private collection

Freud has painted an amazingly various array
of flowers and plants over the years, from spiky
cactuses, potted palms and a banana tree early
on to his large, late pictures of the buddleia and
bamboo in his own garden.

as symbols and rhetoric and so on doesn't interest me." Throughout the 1960s,
Freud seemed to be loosening up and tightening his handling according to each
individual image, searching for an equilibrium between painterly risk and fidelity to the subject. The individual hairs of the brushes he used became increasingly visible in the juicy, thickening paint, conveying to the viewer the direction
of each stroke, its pressure, the loadedness of the brush. All this helps to commu-
nicate the energy and mass beneath the sitter's skin, as well as the fluctuating
conditions of the skin itself. Surfaces that other painters might render as whole
and continuous Freud breaks up into patches of close-toned hues, in ways that
can suggest a deliquescing, disordered Cézanne one minute, a more clotted Rembrandt the next.

Not all Freud's shifting attention is directed at the body. His old interest in
the presence and textures of things – plants, fabrics, hair and so on – finds voice
in several startling paintings that suggest the flexibility of the new approach.
In his painting of a spurt of pink cyclamen (ill. p. 38), for instance, the broad
brushwork conveys the flowers' spongy texture but also their alert, gravity-defy-
ing delicacy.

Still, in the mid-1960s it is the body – the female body in particular – that ani-
mates some of Freud's best pictures. The greatest of them is *Naked Girl* (1966,
ill. p. 39). On the face of it, the picture couldn't be simpler, less conceited: a girl
lies down on a bed and the painter paints her. And yet the finished work is full of
visceral contradictions. The girl's pose is at once self-protecting (legs together)
and abandoned (her arms have fallen into place in the most natural, unselfcon-
scious way). Her body is foreshortened, but also tipped up towards the viewer,
since nothing anchors the bed she lies on in a flat, conventionally receding space.

Naked Girl, 1966
Oil on canvas, 61 x 61 cm
Collection of Steve Martin

There is a subtle torque in the rhythms of the girl's body.
The slight differentiation between thighs; the lop-sided-
ness of rib-cage and nipples; and the neck, head and
hands all tilting to one side, combine to produce a sense
of twitching animal liveliness and physical autonomy
in a body that might otherwise seem subjugated,
pinned down.

Wasteground with Houses,
Paddington, 1970–1972
Oil on canvas,
167.5 x 101.5 cm
Private collection

PAGE 40:
Large Interior, Paddington,
1968/69
Oil on canvas, 183 x 122 cm
Madrid, Museo Thyssen-
Bornemisza

The girl is seen from above
and seems pinned to the floor
(note the loose bulge in her
lower cheek, reinforced by
the heavy vertical sag of the
hanging overcoat). The plant,
by contrast, extends itself
effortlessly into space.
The tension between the
two creates a powerful up-
and-down dynamic, a kind
of spatial vertigo.

Her straight legs are cropped just below the knee and her pink fleshy sex, squeezed between two thick, sallow thighs, is exposed. Exposed and yet not inviting in a salacious way – just there. It is what it is.

The picture is frank, bold – almost like a dare – and 'sauceless' in a way that Freud has gone on to make utterly his own: it is truly a 'naked portrait', as opposed to a nude. It "bypasses decorum," as Robert Hughes once said of another Freud picture, "while fiercely preserving respect." There is no revolted prurience, in the manner of Otto Dix's Weimar prostitutes, and no sexual anxiety, in the manner of Stanley Spencer's Leg o' Mutton nudes.

Floorboards enter into Freud's pictures in the late 1960s, most noticeably in *Large Interior, Paddington* (1968/69, ill. p. 40). This painting shows a young girl (one of Freud's daughters) lying on the floor beneath a huge, potted plant. The girl is naked but for a singlet, and a dark overcoat hangs on a hook behind her. One feels a new kind of ambition in the picture. The scale is rather grand, and the painting's psychological impact is disorienting. The presence of each separate entity – the girl, the coat, the plant, the pot – is sharply discordant. Coexistence itself is lent an air of unlikelihood.

People, plants, animals, and things: these elements recur in different combinations in most of Freud's greatest pictures over the next three or four decades. There are brief forays out of the house: a horse, for instance, is painted in a stable standing in hay. And for two years, between 1970 and 1972, Freud paints the view out of his window: a wasteground scattered with rubbish and, rising up behind it, the backs of terrace houses, heavily punctuated by pipes and

A Filly, 1970
Oil on canvas, 19 x 26.6 cm
Private collection

chimneys. *Wasteground with Houses, Paddington* (1970–1972, ill. p. 41), is a study in truth and contingency: this thing here next to that thing there; this thing growing, that thing dead; this thing discarded, that thing in use; this thing smooth, that thing rough; things spilled, things contained, all of it closely observed and freshly set down.

In 1970, Freud made a drawing, in pencil, of his father – a tour de force of sinuous arabesques and misaligned volumes that cohere in the mind to produce an image of exhaustion and spleen. In April of that year, while he was working on *Wasteground*, his father died. His mother subsequently fell into depression. "She had tried to kill herself when my father died," explained Freud. "She did a perfectly good job, but she was found by her sister, who lived next door and brought her back to life when she was virtually dead. After that, even though my mother had amazing health and was really fine, she pretended she was very ill. She was just terribly depressed to be still alive when she'd made this decision. I started painting her, because she'd lost interest in everything, including me. Before then, I always avoided her because she was so intuitive that I felt my privacy was rather threatened by her … Since she wasn't interested in me, I had a good model. But then also, I did it to cheer her up, to give her something to do. I got her, or got someone to get her, in the morning, and I did this for eight or nine years before she died. I did a lot of pictures."

So began an extraordinary, uninterrupted series of portraits, over a period of a decade and a half, of an aging woman who happened to be Freud's mother Lucie. "I got her, or got someone to get her, in the morning, and I did this for eight or nine years before she died. I did a lot of pictures." The first two, both painted in 1972, are head portraits. They are close-in, fully resolved studies that reveal Freud's deepening interest in the physicality of the face – the interplay of volumes, surfaces, skin condition and light. More portraits of his mother followed. One, painted in 1973, shows her seated in a chair while Freud's lover at the time reclines naked on a bed behind her. In fact – unusually for Freud – the lover and the mother did not pose together. They had never met – although unbeknownst to either, the one's child was the other's grandchild.

In the pictures that follow, as Lucie's pose loses its formal stiffness, her physical presence becomes more pronounced. In *The Painter's Mother Resting III* (1977, ill. p. 44), for instance, she is seen lying on a bed. Freud shows only her upper torso, covered in a paisley dress; her face, weathered and watchful; and,

The Painter's Mother Resting III, 1977
Oil on canvas, 59.1 x 69.2 cm
Private collection

Freud describes, without sentimentality, the doubled contour of his mother's sagging, jowly jawline, her fiercely empty stare and her thinning grey hair. For the broken capillaries on her cheek, he uses a sort of grey top-soil ploughed back into by the back of the brush. This portrait was one of a long series he painted of his mother in the wake of his father's death.

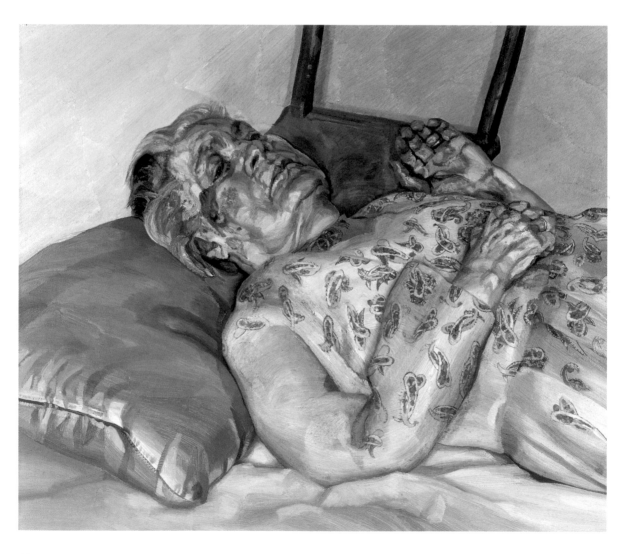

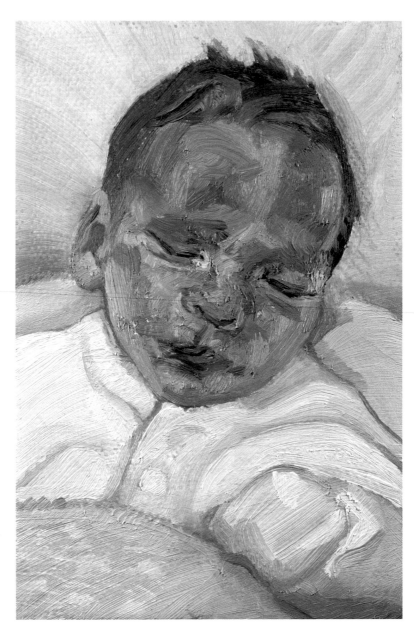

Fred, 1985
Oil on canvas, 17.9 x 12.1 cm
Private collection

The baby, Freud's son, is shown sleeping, but the artist conveys how effortful and urgent even sleep can be. Being alive, even at its simplest, requires an extraordinary coming together of chance and concentrated purpose. Freud's combination of close-in observation and pasty, scumbled paint pushed and pulled in every direction communicates this to startling effect.

most conspicuously, her hands. Freud once confessed that his sitters' weariness gives him energy. Here it seems true: Lucie's air of surrender seems to be in an inverse relationship to the artist's concentrated scrutiny, his steadfast vigil. His attention is evenly distributed not just over her flesh but over the rigorously repeated patterns of her dress and the bedspread, patterns that seem almost to bind that flesh in place.

Most heads conform to a design notable for its symmetry: two eyes and eyebrows either side of a nose, a centred mouth, symmetrically aligned rows of teeth and two flanking ears. And yet, of course, there are countless specific, unrepeat-

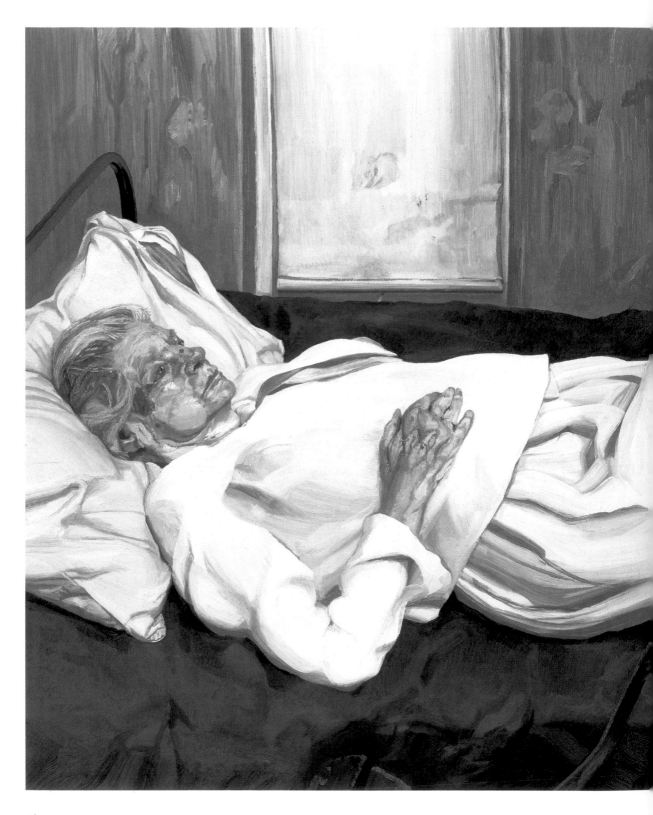

The Painter's Mother, 1982
Etching, 15 x 13 cm
London, Tate Britain

PAGE 48:
Head of a Big Man, 1975
Oil on canvas, 40.9 x 27 cm
Private collection

The man's head seems to tilt, chin first, out of
the picture plane and into the viewer's space,
making for a remarkably unmediated presen-
tation. Note, too, the conspicuous absence of
symmetry and the unevenly squashed, bent
cartilage of the nose.

PAGE 49:
Frank Auerbach, 1975/76
Oil on canvas, 40 x 26.5 cm
Private collection

Auerbach's down-turned face seems dwarfed
by his bulging cranium. It seems scrunched
and recessive, as if concentration alone might
physically warp one's shape, push one away
(which of course it can).

The Painter's Mother Resting, 1982–1984
Oil on canvas, 105.4 x 127.6 cm
Private collection

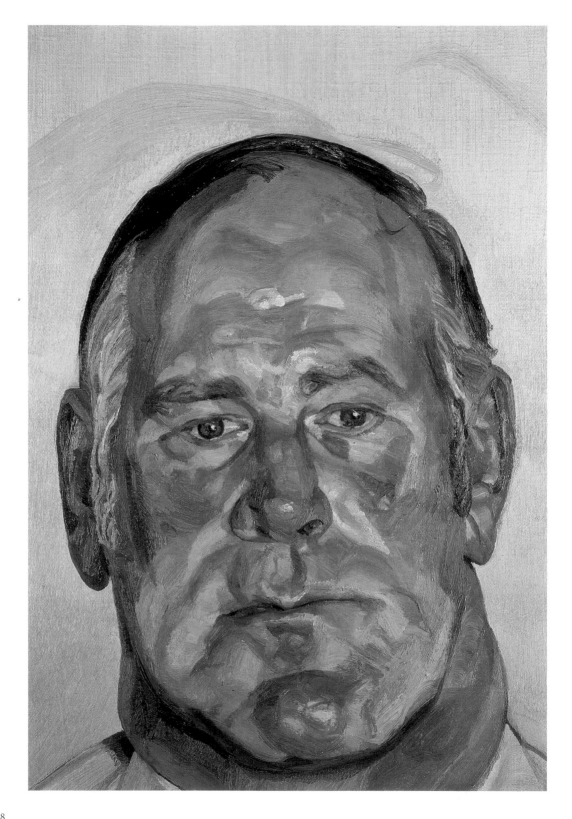

PAGE 51:
John Richardson, 1998
Oil on canvas, 15.7 x 11.4 cm
Private collection

The model, a biographer of Picasso, lives in
New York and could only offer a limited number
of sittings. Freud, whose paintings usually take
between several months and a year and a half to
complete, took up the challenge, producing this
small, surprisingly vigorous work. Its success
gave Freud the confidence to try several more
small portraits from limited sittings, including
his 2000/01 portrait of the Queen.

Man in a Sports Shirt, 1982/83
Oil on canvas, 50.9 x 40.7 cm
Private collection

Freud is renowned for his renderings of flesh,
but he also has an abiding interest in clothes,
hairstyles and other such details. He has painted
silver suits, paisley dresses and T-shirts with
unblinking attentiveness. This moustachioed
man in his sports shirt seems instantly familiar,
utterly strange.

able and unforgettable ways in which actual faces refuse to conform. Lucian
Freud disavows the face's ideal symmetry, revelling instead in the way real faces
and heads are studded with maverick particulars.

Lawrence Gowing sat for Freud in 1980, noting that he "did not draw verifi-
ably from a fixed position, which he could depend on returning to." When Gowing quizzed him about this Freud answered that for him the process "was more
like aiming than copying … I take readings from a number of different positions
because I don't want to miss anything that might be useful to me." Gowing said
he "had the impression of a process rather like echo-sounding."

Between 1974 and 1976, Freud made a series of head portraits that feel like
breakthroughs. They involve no particular formal innovations. But they do suggest a disregard for conventions of portraiture and a degree of involvement that
is freshly disquieting. *Last Portrait* (1976/77, ill. p. 42) is an unfinished painting so
raw and yet so resolute and steady (at least until the moment of leaving off) that
it makes commentary redundant. "Freshly felt emotion can't be used in art without a filter," the artist once said. "It's like people thinking manure is just shit, so

Francis Wyndham, 1993
Oil on canvas, 64 x 52 cm
Private collection

they shit in a field and they think the shit will feed the plant. In fact it half-kills it." Why did Freud leave off painting *Last Portrait?* Either because his sitter refused to continue, or because the emotion attached to her was no longer possible to filter. In either case, the result is upsetting, disruptive, lovely.

Head of a Big Man (1975, ill. p. 48) makes for a remarkable contrast. This thick-necked, indelicate, pink-fleshed businessman was the subject of several of Freud's most powerful paintings of the period. Here, his sweaty chin and jowls seem disproportionately large, his blue unfocussed eyes quite small. The same year, Freud painted his friend, the painter Frank Auerbach (ill. p. 49) and instead of emphasising the chin and jaw, as in *Head of a Big Man,* he now attends to the top half of the head: the large, bulging expanse of Auerbach's brow as it pushes forward and the lively confection of receding hair and oily, light-reflecting scalp. The sense of concentration, of inwardness, is intensely absorbing.

Freud is usually working on at least one head or head-and-shoulders portrait at any given time. He has painted his son Fred as a baby (ill. p. 45) – an astonishing rendition of the effort and animation that can play across even a sleeping baby's face – and he has painted the Queen (ill. p. 53). He has painted old friends such as Francis Wyndham (ill. p. 52), the writer, and Robert Fellowes, the Queen's secretary. He has painted girlfriends and grandchildren. He has painted his brother Stephen, his friend and assistant David Dawson, his several daughters, and his dealer William Acquavella. None of these portraits is fundamentally different from Freud's other paintings. They are approached the same way, with the same interest in particularities, the same refusal to idealise. But viewed apart, it is clear that they qualify as one of the most impressive bodies of portraiture in the history of art. Superficially, they may seem traditional, but they retain a shock that familiarity cannot blunt. It is hard to account for. Doubtless it has everything to do with Freud's handling of paint, which combines bravura passages with moments of awkward urgency. But it also reflects his determination to respond with patient alertness to each of his sitters as individuals. Always, he seems to get across the heft and weight of each head, and then something else: something to do with the tremendous effort involved in simply being, in having this skull and these eyes and this mouth and this flesh (all invisible to oneself) act as one's own chief representative.

PAGE 53:
Portrait of Her Majesty the Queen, 2000/01
Oil on canvas, 23.5 x 15.2 cm
The Royal Collection

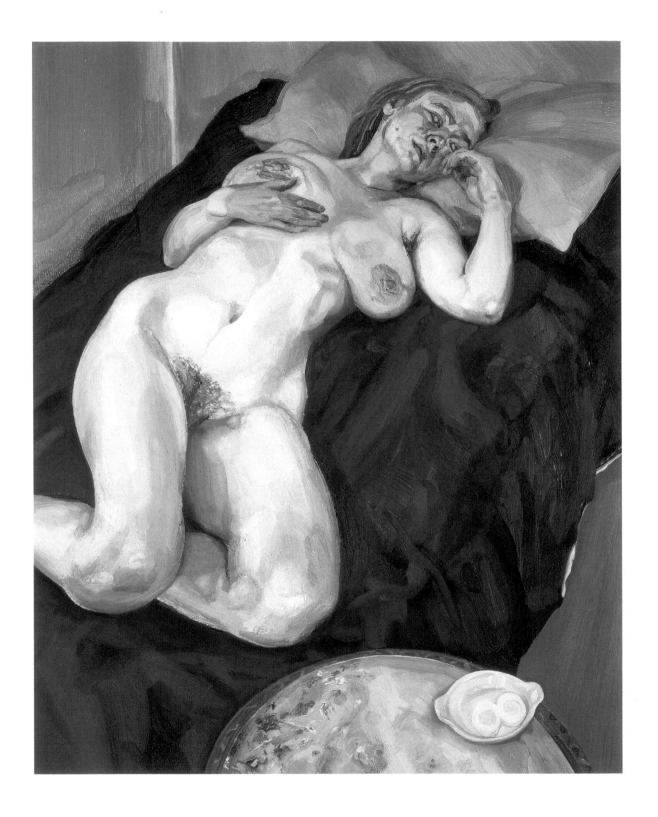

Biology

From the mid-1970s, Freud began to use Cremnitz white – a paint heavy with lead oxide – to convey more powerfully the texture and solidity of flesh. He proceeded, over the next decade, to turn out a series of paintings of naked women (and one or two men) that are unprecedented in the long tradition of the nude. They show women reclining on couches with exposed breasts and genitalia; and yet they are not intended to titillate. (Despite this, they are often erotic, in the wider sense of ample, fecund, charged with physical promise.) They show the wear and tear of occupying a body: sagging breasts, blemished skin, veins, rashes, pits and protuberances. And yet there is no note of disgust or revulsion. In almost every case, the sitters seem comfortable and relaxed. In some cases they are sleeping – never more touchingly so than in *Naked Portrait* (1980/81, ill. p. 60), perhaps the greatest ever painting of a heavily pregnant woman. "Freud," wrote Michael Podro, "would hardly admit to any overarching project or ideology, but what is bound up in his painting is a battle against unspecific, sanitized sexual fantasy and its correlate, prettified art."

Girl with Closed Eyes, *1986/87*
Oil on canvas, 45.9 x 58.7 cm
Private collection

Several of these and later naked portraits depict Freud's grown-up daughters – Annie, Alice, Rose, Ib, Susie, Bella and Esther. In *Rose* (1978/79, ill. p. 59), the artist has used every means at his disposal to get across not just the look but the feel and the sensation of occupying her particular body. The sheet stretched tautly between her legs seems to tether the painting to a narrower slice of time than is usually the case in Freud's portraits: the sense of stretch and expansion is palpable. The twenty-year-old model, in William Feaver's lovely, apt phrase, "confidently yields bodily sensation."

Asked in 1991 whether painting his daughters made things in any way "extreme", Freud told Leigh Bowery: "My naked daughters have nothing to be ashamed of." To John Richardson, he said: "I paint only the people who are close to me. And who closer than my children? If I had thought it odd to paint them, I would never have done so. For me, painting people naked, regardless of whether they are lovers, children or friends, is never an erotic situation. The sitter and I are involved in making a painting, not love. These are things that people who are not painters fail to understand. Besides, there's something about a person being naked in front of you that invokes consideration – you could even call it chivalry – on my part: in the case of my children, a father's consideration as well as a painter's."

PAGE 54:
Naked Girl with Egg, *1980/81*
Oil on canvas, 90 x 75 cm
London, The British Council

55

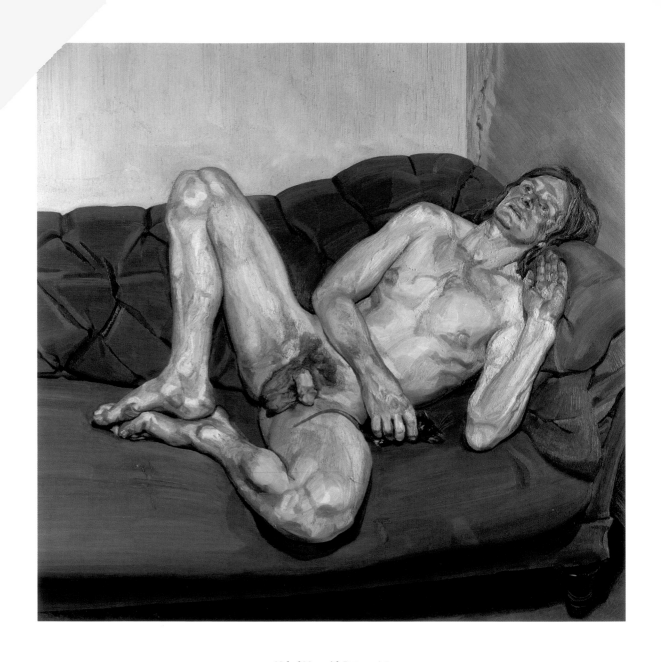

Naked Man with Rat, 1977/78
Oil on canvas, 91.5 x 91.5 cm
Perth, Art Gallery of Western Australia

Naked Portrait with Reflection, 1980
Oil on canvas, 90.3 x 90.3 cm
Private collection

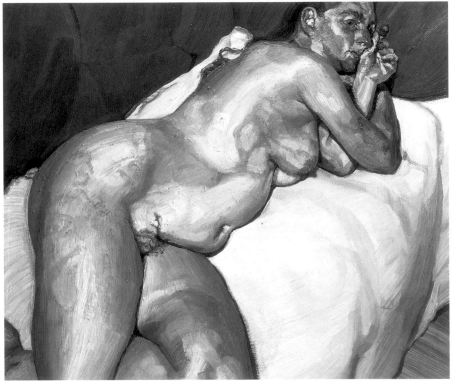

PAGE 60:
Naked Portrait, 1980/81
Oil on canvas, 90 x 75 cm
Private collection

"I'm really interested in people as animals," Freud has said. "Part of my liking to work from them naked is for that reason. Because I can see more. And it's also exciting to see the forms repeating themselves right through the body and often in the head as well. I like people to look as natural and physically at ease as animals, as Pluto, my whippet."

In *Double Portrait* (1985/86, ill. p. 65), the revelation of painted underbelly combines with the dog's tail, testicles, padded paws and claws at the lower right of the canvas to impress upon us the sheer otherness of animal life. The angular hind leg and clawed paw of Joshua, the whippet, just *do not match* the languorously extended arm of his human companion (Freud's daughter Bella) nor the gentle undulations of fabric covering her torso. But at the other end of the painting, things feel rather different. Here, the crimson and pâté-coloured tones of Bella's raw, fleshy face rhyme uncannily with the dog's fur and skin (especially the underbelly). The hook of the leading claw is deliciously consonant with the curl of Bella's right hand. The vein of her right hand rhymes with the smudges of dark colour in the dog's fur. And Joshua's snout in his companion's listlessly open hand is so striking a pose of complicit indolence that one feels one's own body carried along in synergy; one's own hand virtually feels the familiar wetness of the dog's nose. So, while the whole picture jolts the viewer with an electrical charge of otherness, it also induces an awareness of the natural accord between humans and animals in states of rest. Repose here is founded on the shared fact of embodiment.

"The animal is not closed and inscrutable to us," wrote Georges Bataille in *Theory of Religion.* "The animal opens before me a depth that attracts me and is

Annabel Sleeping, 1987/88
Oil on canvas, 38.7 x 56 cm
Private collection

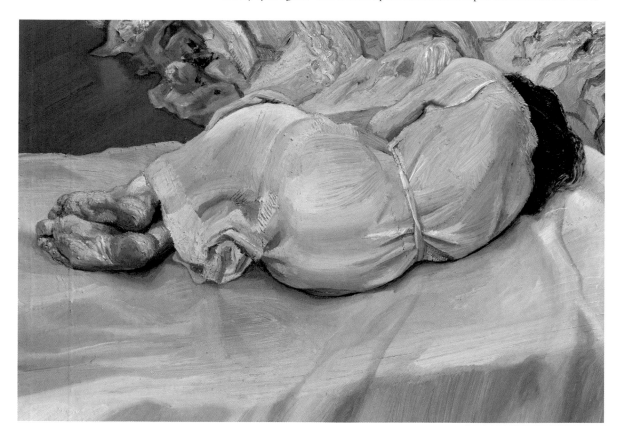

Two Japanese Wrestlers by a Sink, 1983–1987
Oil on canvas, 50.8 x 78.7 cm
Chicago (Il), Art Institute of Chicago, restricted
gift of Mrs Frederick G. Pick; through prior gift
of Mr and Mrs Carter H. Harrison

Naked Man on a Bed, 1987
Oil on canvas, 56.5 x 61 cm
Private collection

Double Portrait, 1985/86
Oil on canvas, 78.7 x 88.9 cm
Private collection

Girl in Striped Nightshirt, 1983–1985
Oil on canvas, 29.5 x 25 cm
Private collection

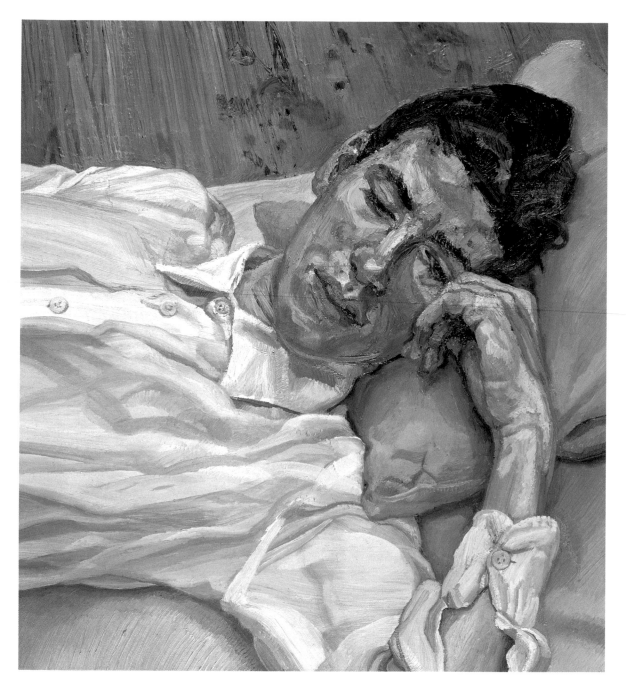

Bella, 1986/87
Oil on canvas, 55.9 x 50.8 cm
Private collection

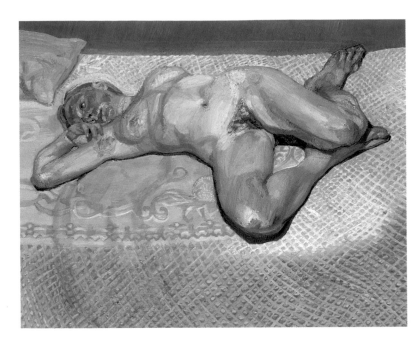

PAGE 69:
Triple Portrait, 1986/87
Oil on canvas, 120 x 100 cm
Private collection

Blond Girl on a Bed, 1987
Oil on canvas, 41 x 51 m
Private collection

familiar to me. In a sense I know this depth: it is my own. It is also that which is farthest removed from me, that which deserves the name depth, which means precisely *that which is unfathomable to me.*"

The early 1980s saw Freud resume etching (ill. p. 47), after a gap of many decades. He will often paint and etch the same subjects, but there is no rule about which will come first, and the results are always very different. The language of etching – the traditionally fine-tuned business of scratching lines into copper, creating grooves which are then bitten into by acid, filled with ink and pressed onto paper – could not, on the face of it, be less amenable to Freud's mature style of painting, which harnesses the visceral energy of paint transferred by loaded brush from palette to canvas. Ordinarily, etching is a medium suited to detailed exactitude and finicky precision – which is exactly why Freud steered clear of it for so many years. The great challenge he set himself when he took it up again was to adapt its inherent aptitude for linear precision to a way of seeing the human body that was already deeply in tune with its sweeping volumes, its surging internal fluids, its ungainliness and its constant, breathing movement, even at rest. He has succeeded marvellously. In ways that feel entirely new to the medium (long, reiterated curving lines, bold, unsystematic cross-hatching and so on) Freud's etchings capture the physicality, the awkwardness and the surprising beauty of the body in states of rest and abandon. In many of them, the supporting surfaces on which his models rest (sofas, chairs, floors, beds) are left out. Cropped, seen from above or seen upside down, they seem to float in the distance or thrust out into our space.

Realism as Theatre

There is a rich and beguiling thread running through art history of artists who have painted portraits of people dressed in costume, pretending to be someone else, but not really *convincingly* pretending. They may be self-portraits or portraits of others. Rembrandt, for instance, painted himself in oriental costume, as the philosopher Democritus, in the manner of Titian's *Portrait of a Man,* and in an array of other fantastic guises – but always, first and foremost, as Rembrandt. He was a master – not just in his self-portraits but in many of his mythological and religious paintings – at building a fictional scaffolding, then encouraging it to fall away in the viewer's imagination.

Just as in Rembrandt you can always feel a dressing-up box just out of frame, in many of Lucian Freud's late pictures the viewer is made to feel acutely aware of the painting's artificial scaffolding. We are made more and more conscious, for instance, of the studio setting. We are shown models leaning or lying against heaped-up piles of paint-stiffened rags (the rags which Freud uses to wipe his brushes). We see thick, encrusted smears of paint on the floorboards and walls; we see sitters' names and phone numbers scrawled on the wall; we see the steps the artist uses to reach high parts of his bigger canvases, and so on. Above all, we are made conscious, through various unexpected means, of what the critic Michael Kimmelman called "the boredom and embarrassment of posing" – what it is actually like, in other words, to serve as a model for a Freud painting. It all adds up to a self-reflexive awareness that is unusual in the history of portraiture (at least to this degree), and Freud makes great play with it.

Throughout the 1980s and particularly in the 1990s, Freud's work became, as he put it, "less autobiographical and, well, more ambitious, I suppose". He painted bigger canvases (and smaller ones). He engaged directly with paintings by the likes of Watteau, Chardin, Ingres, Constable and Cézanne. And he ramped up the degree of self-consciousness in many of his works. These included an extraordinary series of self-portraits (cf. ill. p. 74). (You can't, of course, get much more self-reflexive than a self-portrait.)

Freud has painted self-portraits fairly continuously since 1939, a span outlasted in the history of art only, perhaps, by Picasso. They are both pitilessly direct and full of irony. In many earlier self-portraits – *Reflection with Two Children (Self-Portrait)* (1965, ill. p. 35), for instance – Freud seems to be spying on

Man in a Silver Suit, 1998
Oil on canvas, 110 x 90.6 cm
Private collection

PAGE 70:
Painter and Model, 1986/87
Oil on canvas, 159.6 x 120.7 cm
Private collection

Jean Antoine Watteau
Pierrot Content, c. 1712
Oil on canvas, 35 x 31 cm
Madrid, Museo Thyssen-Bornemisza

Large Interior W11 (After Watteau), 1981–1983
Oil on canvas, 186 x 198 cm
Private collection

This painting is based on an early work by
Antoine Watteau called *Pierrot Content* (1712),
which shows a scene of seduction and jealousy
from the *commedia dell'arte*. Freud's models
roughly adopt the poses of the characters in the
Watteau; they even wear clothes from a dress-up
box. But they sit crammed together, and their
gestures are mute and unconvincing.

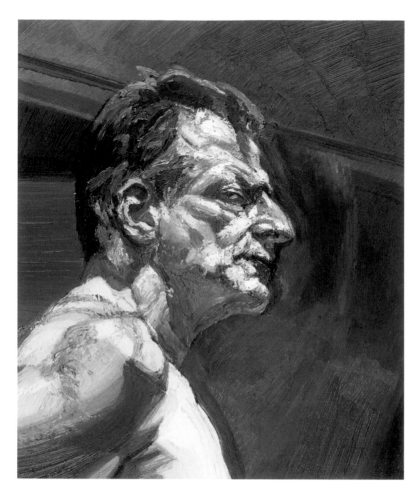

PAGE 75:
Painter Working, Reflection, 1993
Oil on canvas, 101.6 x 79.4 cm
Private collection

The paint is clotted and dry, thickly granulated,
and in some parts applied counter-intuitively.
Around the neck, for instance, in the shadow
cast by the chin, the paint is so thick that it pro-
trudes higher from the surface than the areas
around it.

Reflection (Self-Portrait), 1981/82
Oil on canvas, 30.5 x 25.4 cm
Private collection

himself, as if he were trying to catch his own reflection unawares. His expression
is suspicious, challenging, sceptical. In others, his gaze is direct, frontal, unswerv-
ing. *Painter Working, Reflection* (1993, ill. p. 75) shows the naked painter standing
in nothing but a pair of laceless boots, holding a palette in one hand and palette
knife in the other. There is something resolute in the set of the artist's face,
expressing persistence against the odds – even against good sense. The tone is
heroic, pathetic, both at the same time.

Subsequent self-portraits, such as *Self-Portrait, Reflection* (2002, ill. p. 1) and
Self-Portrait (2004), ratchet up the sense of mortality. Freud's thickening im-
pasto communicates a victory of obscurity over clarity, of deepening uncertainty
over fatuous assumptions about the wisdom of old age. One senses the artist's
own self-conception – prodded and challenged in earlier self-portraits – here
almost gasping for breath, in a way that calls to mind the late self-portraits of
Rembrandt or even Bonnard.

Between 1981 and 1983, Freud worked on a painting called *Large Interior W11
(After Watteau)* (ill. pp. 72/73). The Watteau painting on which it was based – an
early work called *Pierrot Content* (ill. p. 72)– is small. It shows a gormlessly self-
satisfied Pierrot sitting between two women. One of them is serenading him, the

PAGE 76:
Two Irishmen in W11, 1984/85
Oil on canvas, 172.7 x 142.2 cm
Private collection

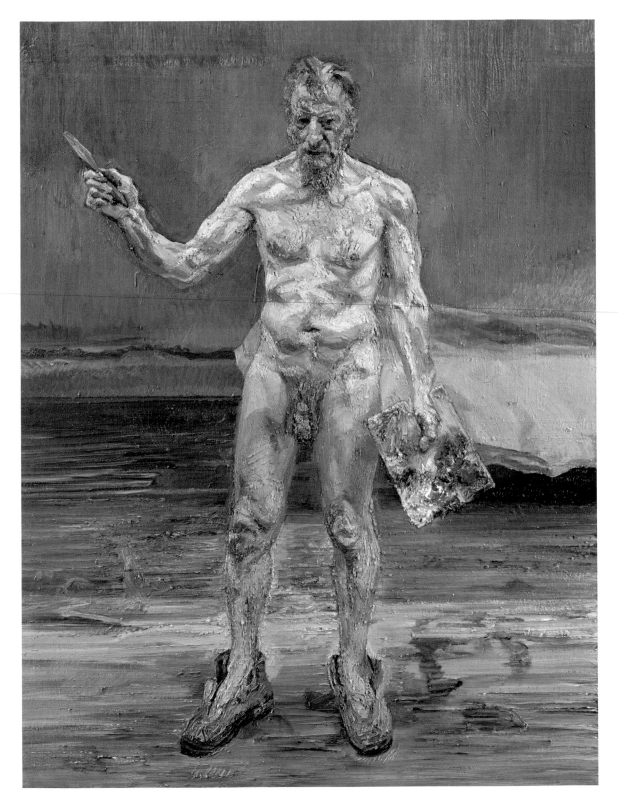

And the Bridegroom, 1993
Oil on canvas, 232 x 196 cm
Private collection

Leigh Bowery, an Australian performance artist whom Freud befriended in the 1990s, is shown here reclining beside Nicola Bateman. Bateman designed Bowery's inventive, provocative costumes and, shortly before his death from an AIDS-related illness, she married him. The title is from a poem by A. E. Housman: "And the bridegroom all night through / Never turns him to the bride."

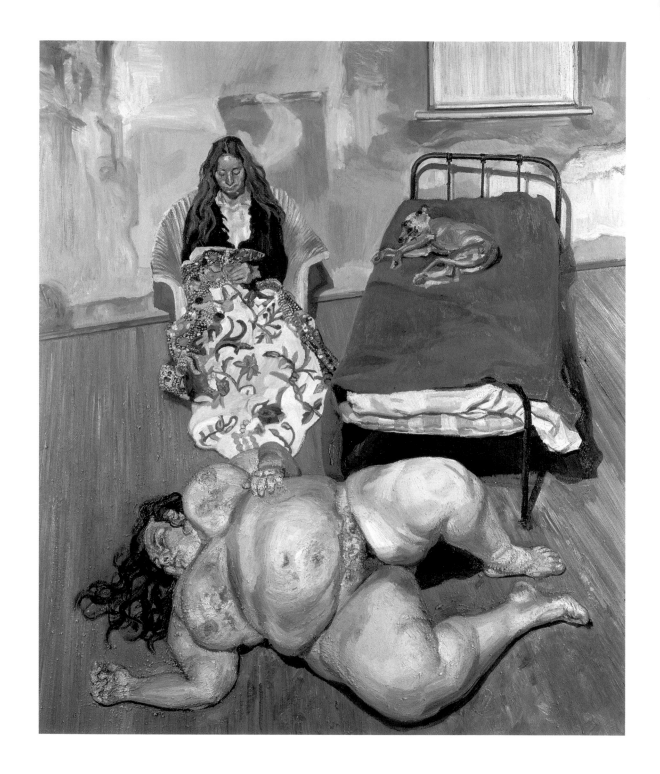

Evening in the Studio, 1993
Oil on canvas, 232 x 196 cm
Private collection

Benefits Supervisor Sleeping, 1995
Oil on canvas, 150 x 250 cm
Private collection

other looks sulky and jealous. Two other figures round out the scene, which is based on the *commedia dell'arte*. Freud's picture expands and monumentalises the original scene, but at the same time allows all its convention-bound drama to drain away. In the Watteau, each character's gestures are instantly legible. Freud's figures either fail to gesture at all or do so unconvincingly, so that we are made aware of the awkwardness – and the likely discomfort – of 'holding a pose'. Against the gracious dispersal of Watteau's figures, Freud gets his to sit crammed together on a regulation issue iron bed. The setting is no benignly romantic forest, as in the Watteau, but a bare, well-lit room. The only references to 'nature' are the vibrant floral prints on two of the girls' dresses; these stand in counterpoint to the unruly, half-decayed pot plant behind them. The overall execution is heavy, in contrast to Watteau's inimitable lightness.

"It is as though Freud had chosen to rework a painting of the utmost theatricality in order to assert his own mistrust of theatre," wrote Robert Hughes. But of course, there is theatre in it. "For the first time in my life the individuals were secondary to the plan of the painting," Freud told Hughes. "I got them to look at the Watteau; and told them the idea of reworking it; and said I wanted a similar composition. I didn't want period costume, but I wanted variety in the clothes, and that they could dress up a little bit." The Watteau, in other words, functions for Freud as a kind of scaffolding, which is made to fall away in the viewer's imagination by his wilfully unillusioned treatment. The result, paradoxically,

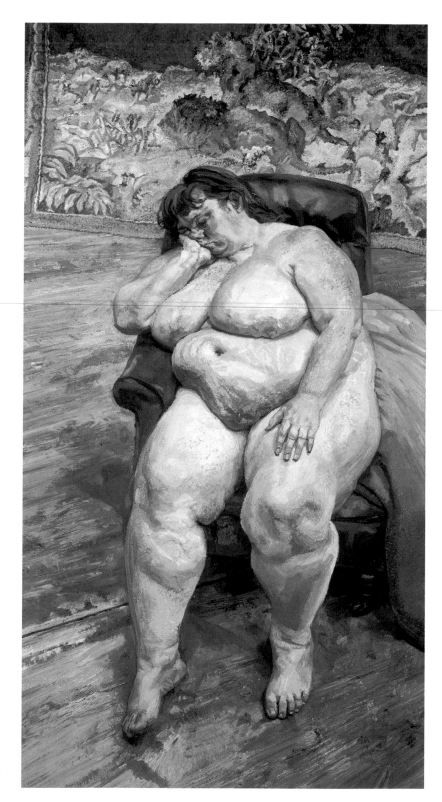

Sleeping by the Lion Carpet, 1996
Oil on canvas, 228 x 121 cm
Private collection

Through Leigh Bowery, Freud met Sue
Tilley. He painted some of his most
ambitious portraits of her, including
this one, which shows her asleep on
a chair in front of a hanging carpet
emblazoned with two stalking lions.

PAGE 80:
The Brigadier, 2003/04
Oil on canvas, 223.5 x 138.4 cm
Private collection

The sitter is Andrew Parker-Bowles, an
old riding friend of the artist. He wears
his uniform (he is a former command-
ing officer of the Household Cavalry),
but it is casually unbuttoned, revealing
a generous paunch. James Tissot's portrait of Frederick Gustavus Burnaby in
the National Portrait Gallery, London,
seated and wearing long red-striped
trousers, was a sort of joking inspiration
for this huge, surprising work.

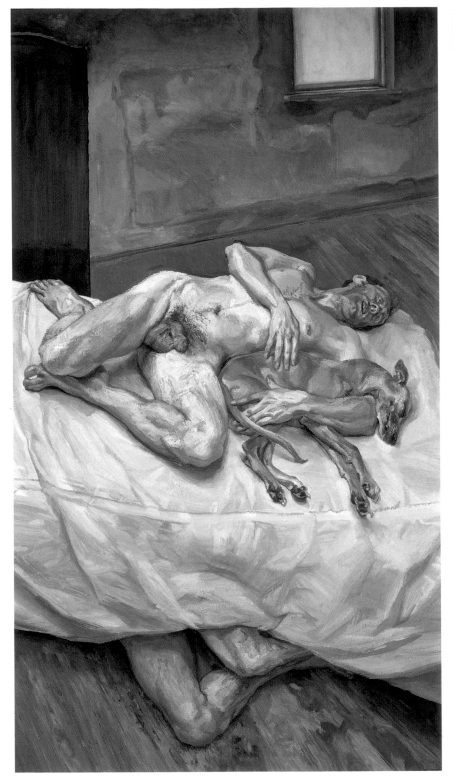

PAGE 83:
Pluto and the Bateman Sisters, 1996
Oil on canvas, 175 x 135 cm
Private collection

Sunny Morning, Eight Legs, 1997
Oil on canvas, 234 x 132.1 cm
Private collection

Freud's assistant and regular model, David Dawson, himself a painter, is shown lying on a bed with his arm around Freud's whippet, Pluto. Dawson's legs are repeated at the bottom of the canvas, emerging from beneath the bed. Freud had planned on putting shoes there, but decided he needed something animate instead.

Woman with Eyes Closed, 2002
Oil on canvas, 30.5 x 20.3 cm
Private collection

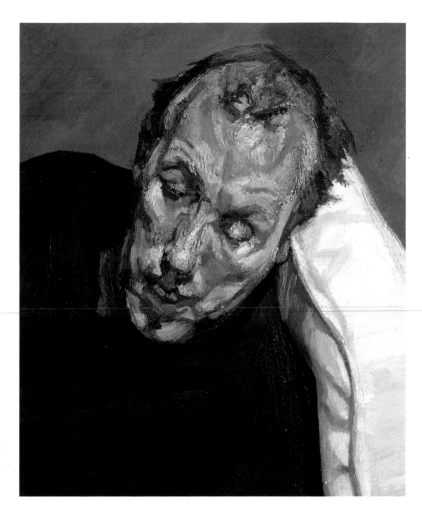

David, 2003
Oil on canvas, 56.2 x 46.5 cm
Private collection

Freud has painted the face and body of his
assistant David Dawson more, perhaps, than
any other sitter. This portrait places us in close
proximity to him, but from an angle that makes
it difficult to fix our own position in space.
The effect is to emphasise his closeness and
vulnerability. He seems either oblivious or
trustingly unconcerned.

is that the sitters are freed from any constructed fiction – not just Watteau's theatricality but also Freud's own realism – and graced with a new depth of human
freedom. They become "unreally alive" and, strange to say, more humanly plaus-
ible. *After Watteau,* admitted Freud, was "slightly costumy". But "I didn't try and
forget who they were, and in the end they are just *there*."

One sees precedents for Freud's treatment of the Watteau in pictures like
Velázquez's *Mars,* in the Prado. Instead of some heroic and muscular incarnation
of bellicosity, Velázquez paints the god of war as a decrepit, aging man in a loin-
cloth, his eyes cloaked in the shadow of his absurd helmet, his post-coital exhaustion comically evident. Corot's portrait, *Man in Armour,* in the Musée d'Orsay,
is another example. This man sits, bored and defeated, in what is clearly a studio:
he is about the least daunting warrior in the history of art. One could point also
to Manet's picture of Victorine Meurent as a bullfighter, or Matisse's paintings
of modern French girls who have raided his dressing-up box in order to fit themselves out as North African odalisques. For all these artists, as for Freud, realism
could often mean a quickening and intensification of self-consciousness and artifice, rather than an easing off – and in this lies the paradox of their art.

In later works such as *Painter and Model* (1986/87, ill. p. 70), *After Cézanne* (1999/2000) and the recent *The Painter Surprised by a Naked Admirer* (2006), Freud continues to play with degrees of artifice, self-consciousness and humour. His purposes are different in each case, but the combination of ambition and irony is inevitably exciting. Undoubtedly, *After Cézanne,* which was bought by Australia's National Gallery in 2001, is one of the most awkward of all his pictures – not only in its unusual shape but in its very conception. Like Freud's other work, *After Cézanne* insists on the unadorned truth of the studio situation (we immediately, for instance, recognise the bare walls of the artist's studio and the portable steps, and may even recognise the models – one of whom is the artist's son – from previous Freud paintings). But it also describes actions bordering on melodrama: a knocked-over chair, a turning away, a comforting gesture, the entrance of a third person. The implied story derives, as the title indicates, from several small paintings by Cézanne called *Afternoon in Naples.*

The studio situation, the hint of melodrama, the borrowing from Cézanne: Freud seems to want us to keep all these threads in play at once, and he wants us

TOP:
John Constable
Study of the Trunk of an Elm Tree, c. 1821
Oil on canvas, 30.6 x 24.8 cm
London, Victoria & Albert Museum

PAGE 87:
Garden, Notting Hill Gate, 1997
Oil on canvas, 149 x 120 cm
Private collection

Freud's paintings and etchings of his garden have formed a major part of his oeuvre. They are partly inspired by his love for Constable. Discussing this painting, Freud said: "I thought rather early on that there would be more dark, shadowy bits, but I realised later that I could sustain the drama that I wanted in the picture by – as I nearly always do – giving all the information that I can."

After Constable's Elm, 2003
Etching, 31 x 24 cm
Private collection

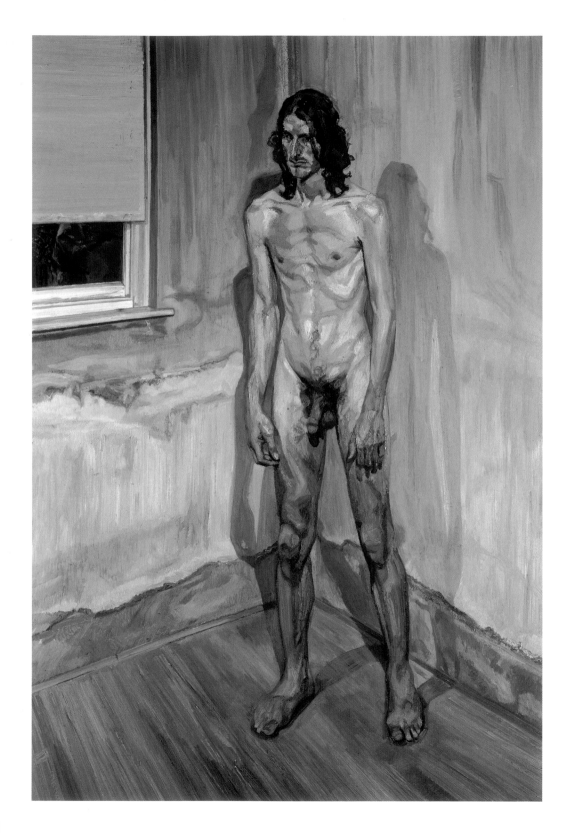

David and Eli, 2003/04
Oil on canvas, 162.5 x 174 cm
Private collection

PAGE 88:
Freddie Standing, 2001
Oil on canvas, 248.9 x 172.7 cm
Private collection

to do so, I suspect, with a sense of humour. Is the painting an erotic anecdote or allegory, as it seems to be in Cézanne? If so, what sort of twist might Freud have given it? What do his handling of the paint, the degree of realism, the changes in composition, and the vastly increased scale do to the way we think about it? There is no fixed answer – the confusion remains beguilingly alive. But the picture is slyly witty, fittingly awkward (since the wit seems to relate to male sexual failure), and thrillingly ambitious.

Freud's naked portraits of women are more often remarked upon than his naked portraits of men, for all sorts of reasons. But the male images are, in their own way, unprecedented. The degree of honesty Freud extends to them – the lack of stereotypical exaggeration, either in the direction of masculine heroics or of pathos – is extremely rare in the history of art.

Often asleep and seen from unusually exposed angles, his naked male subjects are surrounded by an aura of intimate vulnerability. We see this man's hairy thigh, that man's oily scalp, and the sweaty sag of this man's scrotum. But just as often Freud goes beyond mere vulnerability. In the portraits of Leigh Bowery, for instance (ill. p. 77), we detect a surprising, often theatrical degree of bodily confidence. In others, we apprehend not so much vulnerability as the gorgeousness of oblivion or the ambivalent sweetness of physical and psychological trust.

"I really liked modelling, and the things that went with it," wrote the poet Angus Cook, who sat for both paintings and etchings by Freud in the mid-1980s: "cash, prestige, friendship… and it was nice to have someone to watch over me." That someone, he explains, was, in one sense, himself: "to model for a painting was to witness the involuntary disclosure of my self, to observe within me the resistance to stillness (pulse, breathing, blinking etc) by which life goes on." Freud has the ability to capture, wrote Cook, "the alertness of a certain kind of sleep." Looking, we sense a potential movement, and the resulting suspense is "one of the ways in which the reserves and surprisingness of people is emulated in the portraits."

Like Rodin before him, Freud is continually finding new and untried ways to enhance, accentuate, or redouble the immediacy of his images. He will go to extraordinary lengths, try anything. In *Sunny Morning, Eight Legs* (1997, ill. p. 82), for instance, he inserted an extra pair of legs beneath the bed on which the model and dog recline. "I thought I'd have some shoes or clothes under the bed," he said, "but then realised I had to have something more organic there, something moving." The result, he has said, is like a visual stutter – disturbing, unexpected, but in its sincerity, entirely convincing. One thinks of Rodin's *Three Shades,* where the intensification realised through repetition needs no external rationale. "The harder you concentrate," as Freud has said, "the more the things that are really in your head start coming out."

In the 1990s Freud met the Australian performance artist Leigh Bowery. Bowery was already notorious for his outrageous performances and provocative guises. Freud became fascinated by his body. "The way he edits his body is amazingly aware and amazingly abandoned," he said. Bowery brought to Freud's studio a new sense of scope and ambition. *And the Bridegroom* (1993, ill. p. 77), which shows him asleep on a bed with the costume designer and (later, just before his death) Bowery's wife, Nicola Bateman, is a masterpiece of the period. The performer's body, so broad and bullish, so game for anything, is shown stretched out in somnolent repose, the head turned away. The contrast with Bateman's smaller, whiter, more vulnerable figure, facing the other direction but with her two feet touching his thigh, is charged with tenderness and a kind of poignant irreconcilability. (The picture's title is taken from A. E. Housman's poem 'A Shropshire Lad': "And the bridegroom all night through / Never turns him to the bride.")

Through Bowery and Bateman, Freud was introduced to Sue Tilley, a benefits supervisor of great physical proportions. She sat in the mid-1990s for several of Freud's most astonishing paintings, including *Benefits Supervisor Sleeping* (1995, ill. p. 79) and *Sleeping by the Lion Carpet* (1996, ill. p. 81). Freud has said: "I don't want to use the fact that someone might be made differently as a point of interest. I'm not interested in doing freaks. Rather, I've wanted to paint ordinary bodies with the attention freaks might get if they appeared in public." But he admits: "I have perhaps a predilection towards people of unusual or strange proportions, which I don't want to over-indulge."

Throughout this period and in the early years of the new century, as Freud entered his eighties, he painted some of the most ambitious paintings of his ca-

"There is a distinction between fact and truth. Truth has an element of revelation about it. If something is true, it does more than strike one as merely 'being so.'"

Lucian Freud

Expecting the Fourth, 2005
Oil on canvas, 10.2 x 15.2 cm
Private collection

Freud has painted pregnant women on several occasions, on big canvases and on small and always from different angles. This painting is one of his smallest.

reer. Alongside these grand-scale pictures he continued to paint many smaller and arrestingly intimate portraits – for example, *Man in a Silver Suit* (1998, ill. p. 71), *Frances Costelloe* (2002) and *Woman with Eyes Closed* (2002, ill. p. 84). He painted and etched a number of distinctive and moving depictions of animals – *Skewbald Mare* (2004), *Grey Gelding* (2003), *Eli* (2002) – and worked on a continuous series of paintings and etchings of his garden.

Two Plants, painted between 1977 and 1980, was a forerunner to these later garden pictures. In it, dead leaves, living ones and the spaces between things are all attended to with utmost concentration. The later works, such as the etching *The Garden in Winter* (1998/99), or the painting *Garden from the Window* (2002), pursue a similar course, but the handling is broader and grittier and the sense of mortality more subtly pervasive, like water seeping into leaves and earth.

Always operating outside the main currents of 20th-century art, Freud has nonetheless been one of the most influential painters of the past half century. At different times, his example has been claimed by different groups, different movements, different individuals, as a beacon or inspiration. But in the end, Freud's work is hard to claim, because it is so stubbornly resistant to categorisation. His approach does not easily qualify as a 'style' or a 'manner', for it is too much the outgrowth of individual consciousness and character. In the end, each of his pictures is what it is.

"What do I ask of a painting?" Freud once wrote. "I ask it to astonish, disturb, seduce, convince."

Note: quotes from the artist taken primarily from his conversations with William Feaver, but also with Robert Hughes, Leigh Bowery, John Russell and the author.

Lucian Freud
Chronology

1922 December 8: Lucian Freud is born in Berlin to Jewish parents. His father, Ernst, is an architect, and the youngest son of Sigmund Freud, the father of psychoanalysis. His mother, Lucie, is the daughter of a grain merchant.

1933 Freud moves with his family to Britain. They emigrate voluntarily, not as refugees. He goes to school at Dartington Hall in Devon, Dane Court, and Bryanston in Dorset.

1938 Sigmund Freud arrives in London following the Anschluss with Austria.

1939 Freud studies for a term at the Central School of Arts and Crafts in London, then at the East Anglian School of Painting and Drawing, run by Cedric Morris and Arthur Lett-Haines, in Dedham. Has drawings published in *Horizon,* the periodical edited by Cyril Connolly. He becomes a naturalised British subject. His grandfather Sigmund dies.

1940 Spends the winter drawing in Wales with his fellow art student, David Kentish, and later, Stephen Spender, the poet.

1941 Serves in the Merchant Navy on a North Atlantic convoy. He falls ill, is invalided out and returns to Morris's school at Benton End in Suffolk.

1942 Exhibits drawings at the Alex Reid and Lefevre Gallery, London.
1943 Moves to Paddington in London.

1944 Has his first solo show at Alex Reid and Lefevre Gallery, London.

1946 Spends two months in Paris and then five months on the Greek island of Poros.

1947 Shows at the London Gallery.

1948 Marries Kitty Garman, the daughter of Kathleen Garman and the sculptor Jacob Epstein. Exhibits again at the London Gallery.

1949–1954 Works irregularly as a visiting tutor at the Slade School of Art.

1950 Exhibits at the Hanover Gallery, London.

1951 Wins Arts Council of Great Britain prize for *Interior in Paddington*.

1952 Exhibits at the Hanover Gallery, London.

1953 Marries Caroline Blackwood.

1954 Freud is chosen, along with Francis Bacon and Ben Nicholson, to represent Britain at the 27th Venice Biennale. "Some Thoughts on Painting", by Freud, is published in *Encounter* magazine in July.

1958, 1963, 1968 Exhibits at Marlborough Fine Art, London.

1970 Freud's father, Ernst, dies.

1972 Completes the first in a series of paintings of his mother.

1972, 1978, 1982 Exhibits at Anthony d'Offay Gallery, London. He is subsequently represented by James Kirkman, until 1992.

1974 First retrospective, Hayward Gallery, London, and touring.

1977 Moves to Holland Park, West London.

1979 Exhibits at the Nishimura Gallery, Tokyo.

1981 Exhibits in *A New Spirit in Painting*, Royal Academy of Arts, London and *Eight Figurative Artists* at the Yale Center for British Art, New Haven, USA.

1982 Lawrence Gowing's monograph, Lucian Freud, published by Thames & Hudson. Freud returns to etching after a break of several decades. Makes 15 etchings in this year alone.

PAGE 92, LEFT:
Lucian Freud's father, Ernst Freud (left), Martin Freud and Sigmund Freud, 1916

PAGE 92, RIGHT:
Lucian Freud's mother, Lucie Brasch, 1919

TOP:
Leigh Bowery posing for *Naked Man, Back View*, 1992, photograph by Bruce Bernard; © Estate of Bruce Bernard

1983 Created Companion of Honour.

1987 Selects favourite works in the collection of the National Gallery in London for *The Artist's Eye,* which shows at the gallery.

1987/88 Retrospective organised by the British Council at the Hirshhorn Museum and Sculpture Garden, Washington, DC. It is his first major exhibition outside Britain, and it tours to the Musée National d'Art Moderne, Paris; the Hayward Gallery, London; and the Neue Nationalgalerie, Berlin.

1988 Exhibits etchings 1982–1988 at Rex Irwin Art Dealer in Sydney, Australia.

1989 Freud's mother, Lucie, dies.

1990 The Australian performance artist Leigh Bowery begins sitting for Freud.

1991–1993 The exhibition *Lucian Freud, Paintings and Works on Paper 1940–1991,* organised by the British Council, shows at the Palazzo Ruspoli, Rome, and tours to the Tate Gallery, Liverpool; the Tochigi Prefectural Museum of Fine Arts; the Otani Memorial Museum, Nishinomiya; the Setagaya Art Museum, Tokyo; the Art Gallery of New South Wales, Sydney; and the Art Gallery of Western Australia, Perth.

From 1992 Represented by William Acquavella, New York.

1992 An interview with William Feaver is published in the *Observer,* just before Freud's 70th birthday.

1993 Awarded the Order of Merit. An interview with Leigh Bowery is published in *Lucian Freud: Recent Drawings and Etchings,* Matthew Marks Gallery, New York (essay by Angus Cook).

1993/94 The exhibition *Lucian Freud: Recent Work* is shown at the Whitechapel Art Gallery, London. It tours to the Metropolitan Museum, New York; and the Museo Nacional Centro de Arte Reina Sofia, Madrid.

1994 A selection of his paintings is hung at the Dulwich Picture Gallery, London.

1995 The exhibition *From London: Bacon, Freud, Kossoff, Andrews, Auerbach, Kitaj,* organised by the British Council, shows at the Scottish National Gallery of Modern Art, Edinburgh, and tours to Luxembourg, Lausanne,

Freud painting HM Queen Elizabeth II, 2001, photograph by David Dawson; © David Dawson, courtesy of Hazlitt Holland-Hibbert

and the Fundació Caixa de Catalunya, Barcelona. *Bacon–Freud: Expressions* shows at the Fondation Maeght in France.

1996 Shows at the Abbot Hall Art Gallery, Kendal, and Acquavella Galleries, New York.

1997 *Lucian Freud: Early Works* shows at the Scottish National Gallery of Modern Art, Edinburgh.

1998 The exhibition *Lucian Freud: Some New Paintings* is shown at the Tate Britain, London.

2000 Shows recent work at Acquavella Galleries, New York. Exhibits new work in response to Chardin's *The Young Schoolmistress* in *Encounters: New art from old* at the National Gallery in London.

2001 Donates portrait of the Queen to the Royal Collection. *Lucian Freud: Naked Portraits. Werke der 40er bis 90er Jahre,* Museum für Moderne Kunst, Frankfurt/M.

2002 The exhibition *Lucian Freud* shows at Tate Britain in London and tours to the Fundació "la Caixa," Barcelona, and the Museum of Contemporary Art, Los Angeles. Freud selects a show of works by John Constable for an exhibition at the Grand Palais, Paris.

2004 Recent work is shown at the Wallace Collection, London, and Acquavella Galleries, New York.

2005 An exhibition, *Lucian Freud,* goes on show at the Museo Correr in Venice during the Venice Biennale.

Lucian Freud working at night, 2005, photograph by David Dawson; © David Dawson, courtesy of Hazlitt Holland-Hibbert

2006 Shows with Frank Auerbach at the Victoria and Albert Museum, London, and at Acquavella Galleries, New York.

2007 The exhibition *Lucian Freud* opens at the Irish Museum of Modern Art in Dublin. Curated by Catherine Lampert, it travels on to the Louisiana Museum of Modern Art, near Copenhagen, and the Gemeente Museum, The Hague. *Lucian Freud: The Painter's Etchings* opens at the Museum of Modern Art, New York. The show is complemented by a selection of paintings.

Selected Literature

William Feaver, *Lucian Freud,* Tate Publishing, London, 2002

Lawrence Gowing, *Lucian Freud,* Thames & Hudson, London, 1982

Robert Hughes, *Lucian Freud: Paintings,* Thames & Hudson, London, 1988

Bruce Bernard, *Lucian Freud,* Jonathan Cape, London, 1996

Sebastian Smee, *Lucian Freud 1996–2005,* Jonathan Cape, London, 2005

Craig Hartley, *Lucian Freud Etchings 1946–2004,* National Galleries of Scotland, Edinburgh and

The Fitzwilliam Museum, Cambridge, in association with Marlborough Graphics, London, 2004

William Feaver, *Lucian Freud,* Electa, Milano, 2005

Lucian Freud and Sebastian Smee, *Freud at Work: Photographs by Bruce Bernard and David Dawson,* Jonathan Cape, London, 2006

Sebastian Smee, *Lucian Freud Drawings 1940,* Matthew Marks, New York, 2003

Nicholas Penny and Robert Flynn Johnson, *Lucian Freud Works on Paper,* Thames & Hudson, London, 1988

Lucian Freud, Leigh Bowery and Angus Cook, *Lucian Freud: Recent Drawings and Etchings,* Matthew Marks, New York, 1993

Richard Calvocoressi, *Early Works: Lucian Freud,* Scottish National Gallery of Modern Art, Edinburgh, 1997

Caroline Blackwood, Anne Dunn, Robert Hughes and John Russell, *Lucian Freud: Early Works,* Robert Miller Gallery, New York, 1993

Lucian Freud, *The Artist's Eye,* The National Gallery, London, 1987

Acknowledgement

The author would like to thank Lucian Freud above all, as well as David Dawson, William Feaver, Chris Murray, Petra Lamers-Schütze, Lioba Waleczek, Diana Rawstron, Joanne Sadler, and Tom and Leila Smee.

Photo Credits

The publishers wish to thank the museums, private collections, archives and photographers who granted permission to reproduce works and gave support in the making of the book, particularly Lucian Freud and Acquavella Galleries, New York.

Acquavella Galleries, New York: pp. 1, 24, 51, 52, 71, 75, 77 Scott Bowron Photography, New York), 78, 79, 80, 81, 82, 83, 84, 85, 87, 88; © Estate of Bruce Bernard (Virginia Verran): p. 93 and back cover; Hazlitt Holland-Hibbert, London: pp. 2, 94, 95; Bridgeman Art Library, London: pp. 6, 8, 11, 12/13, 14, 15, 17, 18, 19, 22, 23, 28, 29, 30, 31, 32, 33, 34, 35, 36, 38, 39, 40, 41, 42, 43, 44, 45, 46/47, 48, 49, 50, 54, 55, 57, 58 (top), 58 (bottom), 59, 60, 61, 62/63, 64, 65, 66, 67, 68, 69, 70, 72/73, 74, 76, 86 (top); John Riddy, London: pp. 7, 9, 16, 21, 53, 56, 86 (bottom), 89, 91; © The Munch Museum, Oslo/Munch Ellingsen Group/VG Bild-Kunst, Bonn 2007: p. 37; © The Royal Collection, London: p. 53 and front cover; Tate Britain, London: pp. 10 (© Cedric Morris Estate), 20 (top), 25, 47.